NIGHT OF THE LIVING CUDDLE BUNNIES

NIGHT OF THE LIVING CUDDLE BUNNIES

Jonathan Rosen

Sky Pony Press
New York

First Edition

This is a work of fiction. Names, characters, places, and incidents are from the author's imagination, and used fictitiously.

Sky Pony Press books may be purchased in bulk at special discounts for sales promotion, corporate gifts, fund-raising, or educational purposes. Special editions can also be created to specifications. For details, contact the Special Sales Department, Sky Pony Press, 307 West 36th Street, 11th Floor, New York, NY 10018 or info@skyhorsepublishing.com.

Sky Pony® is a registered trademark of Skyhorse Publishing, Inc.®, a Delaware corporation. Books, authors, and more at skyponypressblog.com

Visit our website at www.skyponypress.com.

10 9 8 7 6 5 4 3 2 1

Library of Congress Cataloging-in-Publication Data is available on file.

Cover design by Sammy Yuen
Cover illustration by Xavier Bonet

Print ISBN: 978-1-5107-1523-3
Ebook ISBN: 978-1-5107-1524-0

Printed in the United States of America

This is dedicated to my dad,
who had always dreamed of writing a book of his own.
I hope this would have, in some small way,
fulfilled that dream.

NIGHT OF THE LIVING CUDDLE BUNNIES

CHAPTER ONE

WHERE THE WHOLE THING STARTS

Like any good story worth telling, or bad one for that matter, mine starts in the mall.

The toy store, to be precise.

Normally, it would've just been another routine family outing, but as I've learned over the years with us, nothing is ever routine. We were on winter break from school, and Mom and Dad were a little behind on their Christmas shopping, for a change—and with it being only a few days away, they were running out of time. It was one of those things where they would follow my sister Abby and me around and take notes on whatever we looked at, and then just like that, those same things would magically appear under the tree on Christmas morning.

At eight years old, Abby never put two and two together.

At twelve, I did.

Mom and Dad were kind of clueless about that sort of stuff, but I never said anything to Abby. One, I didn't want to spoil things for her. Two, if it meant keeping quiet for Abby's sake *and* still getting gifts in the process, then I could play along.

I even made it easy for them. I told them exactly what I wanted. An iPhone. Nothing else. Nothing to plan for, nothing to figure out. An iPhone. They had promised me one for my birthday. Always saying, "When you're twelve, Devin." Well, *that* birthday had come and gone without one. But it was okay. I'm not the complaining type. I even smiled and said thank you for the new shirts and socks they gave me instead.

Yeah, socks. If there was one thing I never wanted to get again as a gift, it was socks.

But that wasn't going to cut it this time. Not for Christmas. If I didn't get an iPhone, there was going to be trouble. And by trouble, I mean that I would probably smile *again*, and say thank you *again* for whatever lame gift they gave me. That's the problem with being the good one. You don't really have it in you to follow through with the threat of bad behavior.

My sister, Abby, on the other hand . . .

Let's just say that when Abby didn't get what *she* wanted, she had perfected the art of the tantrum. And Mom and Dad bought it. Every single time.

In the back of my mind, I'd always had a feeling that Abby knew *exactly* what she was doing. The problem was, I could never prove it. But if tantrum-throwing had been an Olympic sport, Abby would've been a gold medalist.

First her mouth would close, and her nostrils would flare. Then her eyes would narrow into tiny slits. Her glare would penetrate you like daggers through flesh . . . and that's when it would turn *really* ugly.

She would collapse to the floor, like her skeleton had been plucked from her body. She'd contract like a Slinky before somehow melting into a puddle. Her high-pitched shrieks would burst every eardrum within a five-mile radius, until they actually rose by several octaves into something that resembled a silent scream, not detectable by human ears. The only way to know that it was still going on was by the howling of neighborhood dogs.

And my parents?

Well, they would do just about anything, and I mean *anything*, to prevent that from happening. They claim they never spoiled her, but I knew that wasn't true. They did just about everything in their power to avoid the volcanic eruption, which I liked to call, Mount Saint Abby.

That's where we were now, with the countdown to eruption about to begin in . . . three, two, one . . .

"Moooooooooooom!" Abby yelled from one aisle of the toy store, causing several heads to almost snap off from

3

the violent, whip-like reaction as they turned toward the sound of the scream.

Mom rushed over. "What is it, Abby?"

Abby pointed in every direction. Up, down, and side to side on each shelf. "The Cuddle Bunny, Mom! They don't have the Cuddle Bunny. I want the Cuddle Bunny!"

The Cuddle Bunny just happened to be what every other kid in the country also wanted. It was part of the FAB line of toys. FAB stood for Furry Animated Bestie. In reality, it looked just like any other regular stuffed animal, but as the commercials liked to say, it was also soooo much more. A FAB could play music and interact with you. It could walk, it could talk, it could probably make a sandwich if you asked it to. It was your robotic pal. But the most annoying thing about the FAB? That mind-numbing song.

I'm not going sing it for you, because if I did, it would worm its way into your brain and destroy any form of intelligence you might have. It has such power and control over a person that during the course of the day, you would find the lyrics escaping your lips without even realizing what was happening. The thing is, you're powerless to stop it. There have already been several news reports about people who had to be institutionalized because they'd been driven insane by it. I mean, literally insane.

Okay, I made that part up, but it wouldn't surprise me if it really happened. Because that's how annoying a FAB was. And the bottom line? Abby wanted one . . . and they were *nowhere* to be found.

"Well, they don't have any right now," Mom said. "But who knows? Maybe Santa will bring you one for Christmas."

Abby's hands curled into little shaking fists. "But I don't want it at Christmas. I want it now! Let Santa bring me something else for Christmas."

"I'm sure Santa can't wait to bring toys to tantrum-throwing little girls," I said under my breath.

"Moooooooom!"

Mom glared at me. "Devin!"

"Dad!" I said, although I'm not sure why, since he wasn't even in the aisle yet.

A moment later, he wove his way through the throng of holiday shoppers. His face was pale, expressionless. He looked over to Mom and slowly shook his head.

Mom's hand flew to her mouth as she glanced over to Abby and smiled. It was phony and plastic. "Or," she said.

Abby looked up. "What?"

"I was reading somewhere that the Cuddle Bunny isn't really as good as everybody first thought. There've been lots of problems with it. People say that they break easily and all the kids who got one wound up hating them and never playing with them again."

Abby folded her arms. "So, give me theirs."

She was good at this. To her, this was almost like a game, and she hated to lose.

5

I already knew what that meant for Mom and Dad. They had no chance to win.

"Or," Dad said, "Maybe Santa will get you something else that you might enjoy even more."

Abby's face turned red. Her nostrils flared. It looked like Dad's words had finally hit her. *"Santa's not bringing me a Cuddle Bunny?* But I've been sooooo good!"

"Compared to a velociraptor," I said.

Abby stomped her foot and pointed at me. "Mooooooom!"

"Devin!"

"Dad!" I said again, still not exactly sure why, since he didn't help me whatsoever. Instead, he just stood behind Mom, off where she couldn't see him, and shook his head.

I rolled my eyes. I'd been through this scene way too many times before and it was always the same ending. I'll spare you the details of what happened next, but the end result was that our mugshots were now not-so-proudly displayed under the NOT WELCOMED BACK sign taped next to every Helen of Toys cash register.

Okay, that part wasn't true. What was true, though, was the part where Mom and Dad bought Abby over three bags' worth of toys.

I actually wouldn't have minded so much if not for the fact that Abby gave me a little smirk when Mom and Dad weren't looking. As I said, that kid knew *exactly* what she was doing. Unfortunately, Mom and Dad never realized it.

To make matters worse? On the ride home, it was like it none of it ever happened. Abby reverted from evil-genius mode back into eight-year-old kid as she giggled and played with her new toys while Dad went on and on with one of his boring stories about how the mall was going green and recycling their water.

Mom pretended to be interested.

"It's amazing," Dad said. "Soon all malls will be doing this. If not, they should. This is too important of an issue."

Mom was busy staring at her phone. "Yes, dear. It's amazing."

He smiled. "And I helped design it."

"We're all very proud of you," Mom said.

I think Dad expected a bigger reaction than that. The problem was that we'd heard about it a bunch of times already. Every time we went to the mall, as a matter of fact. By now we could all practically recite his recycled water story by heart. I'm sure in Dad's world, working for the town of Gravesend, it was all extremely exciting, but in the Dexter household, it was already old news.

This was the moment where, if I'd had a phone, I would've popped the earbuds in and listened to music to avoid everything else, but since I didn't, I was stuck hearing it all again. Every once in a while, I gave a little "That's great, Dad," to show I was paying attention, but all I really wanted to do was get back home and out of the car. Well, that is, until we actually did get home.

Two things happened when we finally reached our house that were the beginning of everything bad.

The first? That would have to be the moving van—the one right across the street from my house. If the van was the gunpowder, then the second was the spark.

That would be Tommy.

Okay, maybe it's overstating it a little to say that Tommy was the cause of all the problems, but he sure didn't help. Don't get me wrong, for the most part I liked hanging out with him—I'd known him ever since I was born. Tommy is my cousin. We were pretty much thrown together as babies and had been forced to hang out ever since.

Mostly I don't mind, because after all this time, he's become kind of sort of like my best friend, which pretty much speaks volumes about the state of my buddy list. But there is this other thing about Tommy that nobody realizes.

He's crazy.

I don't mean arguing with the voices in your head type of crazy, although I wouldn't swear to it that he didn't. All I knew was that more often than not, whenever I did hang with Tommy, it meant trouble. Usually for me. I'm not saying that I'm an angel, but out of the twenty-three times we'd been given detention in school, I could honestly say that twenty of them were entirely his fault, with the others being at least partially.

Trouble seemed to find him, and somehow I'm always around when it happens. I try to tell Mom about it, but she always talks about how he's family, and family sticks together through thick and thin, and that sort of stuff.

The worst is when she says that I must be exaggerating. That's the one that always gets me. Tommy does a really good job of acting innocent in front of adults. So good, in fact, that nobody seems to believe how much trouble he can be. Not my parents, not his parents, not the teachers, and not even the principal—but I think he's just tired of us always being in his office for something.

The bottom line was, Tommy meant trouble. And that trouble was sitting on his bike in my driveway, waiting for me.

I tapped Dad's shoulder from the back seat. "Dad, quick, pull into the garage and close it behind you. I'm not in the mood for him right now."

"Devin!" Mom said. "That's not nice. He's family."

"Besides," Dad said, "he's right in the middle of the driveway. I couldn't do it without running him over."

"He'll move," I said. "Probably."

Dad shook his head. "I can't take that chance. If he doesn't, my insurance premiums will go way up and I'm paying enough as it is."

I never know with Dad whether he's joking or not, he speaks so seriously. But either way, he slowed down and stopped before reaching the garage. Which meant that I had no choice but to get out of the car and see . . . Tommy.

"What are you doing here?" I asked.

"I came by to see if you wanted to hang out."

"I'm tired, we just got back from the mall."

"Devin!" Mom said. "That's not nice."

Tommy held up his hand. "It's okay, Aunt Megan. I'm not offended. If Devin says he's tired, I'm sure he doesn't mean anything bad by it."

I rolled my eyes. "Oh, brother."

"There's no excuse for being rude." Mom shook her head. "Now, apologize."

"What? I didn't do anything. Dad?" I turned to him for help.

"Can't do anything now, Devin. I'm carrying stuff into the house." He grabbed the bags from Abby and dragged her along inside.

He had been my only shot. I'd have no choice now. I turned to Tommy. "I'm sorry," I mumbled.

Tommy looked at Mom. "I didn't hear him, Aunt Megan."

Mom frowned. "No, Tommy, neither did I."

"Are you kidding me?"

"Devin!" Mom raised her voice, in that not quite a yell, but more than regular speaking tone. It was her signal that she was not to be messed with. She used it often and was good at it.

I sighed. "I'm sorry." I turned to Mom. "Okay?"

Mom turned to Tommy. "Okay?"

Tommy nodded. "Yes, Aunt Megan."

"Good!" she said. "Now I'm going inside. Come in soon for dinner. Would you like to join us, Tommy?"

"I'd love that, Aunt Megan. You're the best cook ever."

"Good grief," I said.

"Why, thank you, Tommy. I'm glad someone around here appreciates me." She glanced at me. "Now, you two go have fun until I call you in, but stay only around the yard, okay?"

"We will." Tommy nodded.

I watched and waited until Mom got into the house before I unloaded on Tommy. "What are you doing here? Didn't I tell you to stay away from me?"

"You meant that?"

"Yeah, I did. That's your problem, you never listen."

"Wait a second. Are you still mad about the other day?"

"You mean when the motorcycle gang chased us across town? No, I'm not mad about that at all. Why would I be?"

"Oh, good," Tommy said. "I was worried you'd be upset."

"Of course, I'm upset!" I said. "A gang, Tommy. A motorcycle gang! What twelve-year-old gets chased by a motorcycle gang? Between that and the police and all the detentions at school! I mean, we must lead the entire county in detentions."

Tommy scowled. "That's ridiculous. There have to be a lot of schools in the county. There's no way to know what's happening in each one."

I rubbed my eyes. I felt my usual Tommy headache coming on. "Seriously, please stop."

Clang!

We turned toward the sound and saw several huge muscular guys carrying things from the moving van into the house across the street.

"Careful!" A much smaller man ran beside them, shouting and waving his arms. His voice cracked. He seemed to be their boss. I knew because he was carrying a clipboard, and from what I've seen, the one carrying a clipboard and doing nothing while giving everyone else orders was usually the one in charge. "You guys break anything, it's coming out of your salaries. Now, hurry up! I promised it would be done by tonight."

"We're going as fast as we can!" one particularly large guy grunted as he helped carry something out of the truck. He backed out, along with four other guys, carrying a massive sized . . . cooking pot? It was maybe four feet around and looked like it was big enough to put up soup for hundreds of people.

One of them groaned. "Who has a pot this big anyway?"

"How should I know?" Clipboard-Man shrugged. "Maybe it's for parties. Whatever, just be careful."

"What's this?" Another mover came into view, carrying a giant ball made from glass. It looked like an oversized marble.

"How should I know?" Clipboard-Man asked. "Just be careful with it."

"What are you, scared?" One of the movers laughed.

Clipboard-Man ran his fingers through his hair. "I don't know. It's just that there's something weird about this one."

"Don't worry, Chief," one of the movers said. "We'll protect you."

The others laughed again.

They carried the pot up the steps of the porch. The front door opened. They went in, but something else came out. It was small, black, and furry. A cat. It slinked along the edge of the porch and stopped.

It turned toward me, and its eyes narrowed.

My heart thumped. Something strange about it.

Tommy tapped my shoulder. "Devin?"

"Yeah?"

"I don't know how to tell you this, but I think you have a witch moving in across the street."

CHAPTER TWO

Guess Who's Coming to Dinner?

You know how sometimes you watch a scary movie and all the clues are right in front of the characters, but they're just too stupid to realize it? Well, that's the way I was feeling then. It wasn't just the cauldron and the crystal ball—it was also this weird sense settling in. All I know is, if this *had* been a movie, I would've been screaming at the top of my lungs for them to get out of there.

Unfortunately, the "there" was Tommy and me holed up in my room, pacing back and forth, trying to figure out if what we had just seen was really what we had just seen. I wasn't sure but was having a very tough time trying to convince myself otherwise, especially because of Tommy, who was staring out the window through a pair of binoculars.

"What are you doing?" I asked. "It's creepy. Why do you even carry binoculars with you?"

"Huh? Oh, I learned a long time ago that you never know when you're going to need them. Especially in this town. Like now for example. This is the best way to spy on a witch. I'd be able to see almost everything, except for that stupid tree in the way." He angled himself, trying to get a better view around the tree that stood right outside my window.

"There are no such things as witches," I said, realizing I was saying it more for my benefit than his.

He lowered the binoculars, turned to me, and scowled. "Really? You can say that after what we just saw?"

I shrugged. "What did we see? We really didn't see anything, just a pot, a glass ball, and a black cat. Big deal. Anybody could have those things. Doesn't mean they're a witch."

"Doesn't mean they're a witch?" His eyes narrowed. "You are very lucky I'm here."

"Why?"

He looked through the binoculars again. "Did you ever hear of Billy Thompson?"

I shook my head. "Who?"

He turned to me slowly. "Billy Thompson was a kid who lived in this neighborhood around twenty years ago, before your time."

"And yours."

He ignored me. "Anyway, Billy Thompson was just like you and me, a regular kid, until one day, a witch moved right next door to him."

I swallowed hard. I hated that every time Tommy told me a story, I didn't know whether to believe him or not. He always seemed so sure of himself. "That's not true," I said.

"Whose story is this?"

"Yours, but—"

"Are you going to let me finish or not?"

I shrugged. "Sorry."

"So anyway, one day Billy goes snooping around, because nobody believes him that a witch lived next door."

"And?"

"And he disappears." Tommy snapped his fingers. "Just like that. And nobody heard about him ever again or remembered that he even existed."

"Wow . . ." I breathed out the word, then thought. "Wait a second . . . but you just mentioned him."

"What?"

"You just said that nobody remembered that he existed, but you just mentioned him. Your story doesn't make any sense."

He frowned. "Why are you trying to ruin the story?"

"I'm not. I'm just saying it doesn't make any sense. It can't be that nobody remembered him, if you're talking about him now."

Tommy waved his hand in front of him. "Never mind. You're confusing me. The point is, Billy Thompson went snooping and disappeared. I think they found, like, human bones in the witch's soup or something like that." He went back to the binoculars.

I thought of the ridiculously large pot I had seen. My leg trembled a little. "I don't believe you." My voice cracked. "There's no such thing as witches."

"Oh, yeah?" He offered me the binoculars. "Take a peek at this."

I took them from him and looked through to see the movers down below. They walked out of the van in single file, each one carrying an armful of—"Brooms?"

"Well?" Tommy said, the smugness clear in his voice. "What do you make of that?"

"I don't know. Maybe she just likes to keep a clean house?"

My door flew open and Mom burst into the room. "Devin, get ready for—Devin! Are you spying on our neighbors with binoculars?"

"No, I—"

"I told him it was wrong, Aunt Megan," Tommy cut in.

I turned to him. "*What?*"

She glanced at Tommy but didn't say anything. She reached out. "C'mon, hand them over."

I held my tongue and placed them in her hand. If Tommy was upset about his binoculars, he didn't show it. He didn't even blink.

"You can't go spying on people with binoculars, Devin." Tommy wrinkled his nose. "It's creepy."

I sighed. "What do you want, Mom?"

"Oh, yes. Dinner is almost ready and I want you to be on your best behavior. I invited the new neighbor."

Tommy whipped his head in my direction.

"What?" I said. *"What did you do that for?"*

"What are you yelling about?" Mom asked. "What's wrong with inviting the neighbor?"

Tommy and I glanced at each other. What could I say that wouldn't make her think I was nuts? I couldn't exactly tell her that I was pretty sure we had a witch living across the street. Finally, I went with, "Because it's not safe to let a stranger into your house. Everyone knows that. What if it's some crazy, psycho serial killer? Have you thought of that? Because then *you* just let them in here to murder all of us." I'm not really good under pressure.

Mom folded her arms and tapped her foot as she stared at me for several moments before speaking. "Did your father let you watch scary movies again? I warned him about this." She glanced toward my door. "He is so going to get it."

"I didn't watch any scary movies!" I said.

"Okay, then I don't know what this is all about, but our new neighbor is coming for dinner, and I want you to behave." She wagged her finger at me. "And that means none of this serial-killer type of talk." She shook her head, turned, and stormed out.

Tommy rushed to my side. "I think your mom's been compromised. We might have to eliminate her."

I shoved him away. "Will you cut it out? You're not elim-inating my mom. And by the way, thanks for the binocular thing. Now she thinks I'm as creepy as you are."

"Who cares about the binoculars?" He pointed out the window. "You have a witch living right across the street from you! Who, by the way, is coming here for dinner, and all you care about is the binoculars? Help me come up with a plan! We don't have much time." He paced the floor back and forth, smacking his hand against his forehead. "C'mon, think."

"Okay, enough! I knew it was a mistake listening to you. You always make it so I'm not thinking clear, and then I'm the one who gets in trouble. You know what? I don't care if she is a witch. I'd rather deal with her than with you any-way. You're nuts."

"Yeah, keep telling yourself that." He tapped his chest. "Then, I'll be the only one alive while she's feasting on your brains tonight."

"Do you even hear how stupid that sounds? That's what I'm talking about. She's not going to eat our brains, and she's not a witch."

"Tell that to Billy Thompson."

"*You made him up!*"

"Let's agree to disagree on that one. The point is that you have a witch coming over, and we need to prepare." He began searching through my room, lifting papers and looking under my bed.

"What are you doing?"

He got up and rifled through my desk. "Do you have any wooden stakes?"

"What are you talking about?"

His face lit up. "Garlic!" He snapped his fingers. "Wait. *I got it!* Silver bullets!"

I ran over to stop him from going through my things. "Are you out of your mind? Where would I get silver bullets? And besides, that's for werewolves."

"Not just."

I pointed to the door. "Please go. I'm begging you."

"You know, I'm trying to save your life here. So maybe you should be thanking me instead of yelling."

"I'd thank you even more if you left."

"Okay, if you tell me right now that there's not even any part of you that thinks she might be a witch, then I'll go. But first, think about this." He started counting off items on his fingers. "The cauldron, the brooms, the crystal ball, and that weird black cat. Still not one part of you?"

I opened my mouth to answer him, but for some reason the words wouldn't come out. As stupid as it sounded, all of it together bothered me. Even scared me a little. I knew in the back of my mind that this was how Tommy always got me, but I had to admit, everything he was saying started to make sense. "I don't know. It's probably nothing."

"Probably? You don't sound convinced at all." He threw his hands out, palms up. "So, how about we prepare? Just in case? If she's not a witch, then no harm done. But if she is, then we'll be ready for her."

I sighed. Anything to get him to stop. "Fine. What do we have to do?"

He clapped. "Yes! You won't regret this."

"I'm regretting it already."

"Okay, first off, where do you stand on holy water?"

"What are you talking about? Who has holy water?"

He scratched his chin. "We'll have to get some. Put it on our list."

"*List?* What list?"

"You have to make a list!" He pointed to my desk and snapped his fingers. "Go on, I'll wait." He watched until I got out a pen and sheet of paper to take notes.

"Okay, I have paper. Now what?"

Tommy paced the room, rattling off items, not even caring whether or not I was paying attention anymore. "Silver bullets, wooden stakes, garlic. Definitely plenty of garlic."

"That's for vampires."

"It works on all evil creatures, don't you know anything?"

I took a deep breath and scribbled it down. "Fine, garlic. Go on."

"Holy water is the best. I'll have to get some on the way home."

"Where do you get holy water?"

He turned serious. "You don't want to know the places I know."

"Oh, brother," I said.

"Stop interrupting me." He banged his head with his fist. "What else do we need?"

Before he could continue, the sound of the doorbell interrupted us. Tommy and I exchanged glances. If his face was anything like mine, I knew how scared I looked.

"What do we do?" I whispered.

"Why are you whispering?"

I shrugged and whispered again, "I don't know."

"Okay, let me think, let me think . . ." He snapped his fingers and pointed to me. "Listen to me very carefully. You're going to go downstairs."

"*Me?* Why me?"

"It's your house! And besides, I'm going to take care of things up here."

"What things?"

"You leave that to me. But I need you to stall before you open the door. I need some time. And no matter what you do, don't invite her into the house."

"Why?"

"She can't enter your house unless you invite her in. She'll, like, burn or something."

I scowled. "That's also for vampires."

"*It's for all evil creatures!*" he yelled. "Now, you have to start trusting me on this. I know what I'm talking about."

"Where'd you get your information?"

He stared at me. "I can't reveal all my sources."

"You're a moron."

"That's another thing that we'll have to agree to disagree on. All I know is, if Billy Thompson had had someone like me in his life, he still would've been here today."

"You made him up."

"I'm not going to argue about this now." He walked over to my door and opened it. "Now, go! But remember, no matter what, don't invite her in!"

I took a step out into the hall and turned around. "Wait a second. You just kicked me out of my own room."

"We don't have time for this!" Tommy said. "Every second you wait is another second the witch gets closer to having Devin stew for dinner. She'll be eating your brains and using your bones to pick her teeth. And remember this, they start with the kids first. Because to them, kids are the tastiest."

I thought a moment. "Well, wouldn't they start with Abby?"

"Yeah, but you'd be next."

"You're three months younger than I am."

"You're wasting time again! Now get down there and stall!" He slammed the door in my face.

As I walked down the stairs, I could hear the sounds of objects crashing in my room. A part of me wanted to let the witch in, so maybe she would eat Tommy, but with each step, I thought about if this were real. Would she kill us right away? Or maybe wait and fatten us up first? I kept trying to remind myself that there were no such things as witches, but it was no use—the seeds of doubt were already planted.

I took the last step and reached the hallway where the front door was. Nobody had answered it yet. Good. Maybe if nobody did, she'd just go away.

Brriiiing! The doorbell again.

What were the chances that nobody had heard that the second time?

"Mooooooooom!" Abby yelled. "Somebody's at the door!"

I winced. Stupid Abby.

Mom rushed into the hall. "What are you doing? Why aren't you opening it?"

"Mom," I said in a hushed tone. "Don't answer it."

"What? Why not?"

"It's dangerous."

She rolled her eyes. "Not this again. I don't know what's gotten into you, but I'm not discussing it while someone's waiting at the door. We'll talk about it later."

"Don't, Mom, I'm telling you, I have a bad feeling about this."

She bent down and touched my cheek. "Sweetie, I think maybe you've been watching too many scary movies."

"I haven't."

"I'm going to let your father have it later. But for now, just listen. We're only inviting a new neighbor, who doesn't

24

know anybody else in this town, for dinner. That's all. Okay?"

Hearing her say it like that made me wonder if I'd been overreacting. Tommy could do that to you. Make you not think clearly. Who knows how many times I'd gotten in trouble because of him? Finally, I nodded. "Okay."

She smiled. "Good boy. Now, let's not keep our guest waiting."

She reached for the door.

CHAPTER THREE

MEETING THE WITCH?

A thousand thoughts went through my mind as Mom reached for the door, many of them having to do with me as the main ingredient in some type of witch-stew. But the thing that was getting to me the most, was just what was I going to do when she opened the door? Stupid Tommy and his stupid plans. He didn't tell me anything. If the neighbor was a witch, I was not at all ready for her. Would she use her magic right away? Maybe she would put me under her spell and make me her slave. A zombie slave, having to eat brains in order to survive. Or maybe she'd put a curse on my family, which would last hundreds of years until someone broke it by having to kiss me and . . . okay, maybe I was getting a little carried away.

Still, I braced myself just in case, when it suddenly occurred to me: I hadn't even seen her yet. Not good. I had no idea what type of witch I'd be facing. Would she be the old, ugly, wrinkly kind? Or maybe young, beautiful, and evil? Wait! It was also possible that she might be the plain-looking one, who was all nice to everyone, and nobody ever suspected her of being a witch until it was too late.

Those were the worst kinds.

Mom placed her hand on the doorknob and turned it.

I watched as, inch by inch, it turned. Another second and we'd be face to face. Another second and I might be dead. My hands were slick with sweat, my mouth dry.

A crack in the door. This was it.

Mom pulled it open to reveal . . . a guy! A skinny, glasses-wearing guy with a thin brown mustache. He wore a brown, button-down shirt with short sleeves and a red-striped tie. The top of his head had only a few strands of hair, which were combed over the side.

Okay, I had to admit, I hadn't been expecting that.

"Howdy!" the man said in a kind of nasal voice. "How are ya? You must be Devin. I'm Herbert Dorfman. My friends call me Herb or Dorf or the Dorfmeister, but nobody ever calls me late for dinner." He chuckled. "Sorry, that was a little humor there. You'll find out soon enough that I'm something of a cutup. I find it helps when meeting new people. Breaks the ice and all, you know what I mean?"

I shook my head. I had no idea what he was talking about.

"As a matter of fact," Herb said, "my friends always say to me, Herb, you should've been one of those stand-up comedy fellas, we always see on the teevee. But no sir, I could never. I'm not a professional or anything like that, I just do it for fun, you know?" He slid his finger up the bridge of his nose to push his glasses up. "Anyhoo, your mom told me a lot about you and I'm pleased as punch that we could meet!" He extended his hand.

"You're a guy," was all I could say.

"Devin!" Mom said.

"Oh." Herb pointed to his face. "That's okay, I guess the mustache gave it away." He laughed.

I thought back to all the time we spent spying on the house next door and realized that we had never actually seen him. Just the movers.

I looked up and realized that he was still standing on the porch. He hadn't come in yet. Wait . . . was Tommy right?

Meanwhile, Mom just stared at him, like she was waiting. She arched her eyebrows.

I had to see for myself. "What are you waiting for?"

Mom whipped her head at me. "Devin!"

"Oh, that's okay." He laughed again. "I guess I was just waiting for an invitation to come in. I'm one of those old-fashioned types."

My eyes widened. That was it. Tommy *was* right. He couldn't come in unless we asked him!

"Oh, sorry." Mom extended her hand. "Won't you please come—"

"Noooooooooo!"

Mom glared at me. *"What is with you?"* She looked back at Herb. "I'm sorry, Herb. I think he watched a scary movie with his father the other night and he's acting a little strange right now."

Herb laughed. "Oh, no apologies necessary. I saw *The Blob* when I was a child, and I don't have to tell you how terrified I was. Well, that was many hundreds of years ago." He laughed again.

Mom laughed too. "You're not *that* old. But anyway, would you like to come in?"

Herb nodded. "Yes, indeedy! I would sure love to." He stepped inside.

My heart sank into my stomach. Everything around me got blurry, then narrowed, like I was in a tunnel, with the only clear thing in the room at the other end of it . . . Herb.

Then just as suddenly—"Take a look at this!" Tommy's voice snapped me out of the fog. Everything came back into focus—and I immediately wished it hadn't.

Out of nowhere, Tommy rushed in and thrust his arm out.

Herb flinched and shot his hands up in front of his face.

I winced.

Tommy held a small pocket mirror up in front of Herb. "Tommy!" Mom yelled.

Herb spread his fingers and opened up his eyes. He blinked several times. "Oh my, did you give me a fright.

29

Do I have something on me?" He leaned over and looked into the mirror. "Well, I'll be." He reached up and brushed off his tie. "Thank you, young fella. That would've been embarrassing to sit through dinner all night with a spot on my tie. I certainly owe you one."

Tommy dropped his arm. "You're a guy."

Herb laughed. "I never thought there'd be so much confusion. I admit I'm no Erik Estrada, but I assure you, I am indeed a man."

"Who?" Tommy asked.

Dad rushed into the room. "What? What's going on?"

Mom placed her hands on her hips. "What's going on is your son and nephew have gone crazy."

"Don't go crazy, boys," Dad said.

Mom frowned.

She introduced Dad to Herb as they walked into the other room.

Tommy stared into the mirror. "Hmmm, I thought for sure that would work."

"That was your big plan? A mirror? That's what you needed to stay in my room for? To bring a mirror?"

"I thought it was a woman."

"What difference would that make?"

"Witches are vulnerable to mirrors."

"No, they're not. And besides, how did you not know he was a guy? You were watching that house through your stupid binoculars. How'd you not see him?"

Tommy shrugged. "I don't know. He never came out. I guess I just assumed it was a woman."

"Okay, again, I don't understand what difference it would have made if it was a woman."

"Mirrors work on women witches. They freeze when they see their reflections."

I shook my head. "No, they don't."

"They do. Witches can't see their reflections in the mirrors. It freezes them and, like, burns their souls or something like that."

"Where do you get your information from, *Scooby Doo*? Anyway, that's for vampires."

"*It's for all supernatural creatures!*" Tommy said.

I sighed. "I don't think you know anything about witches."

He wagged his finger at me. "That's where you're wrong, I know *everything* about this stuff."

"I don't think you do. I think you're just telling me things to get me to go along with you as usual. And where'd you get a mirror? Is that Abby's?"

"No, it's mine. I carry it with me. I told you, you never know what you're going to run into in Gravesend."

"You carry binoculars and a mirror? What else do you have in there?"

Tommy ignored me and started pacing the room. "There's no time for that now. Let me see, a male witch. That means he's a warlock. This complicates things."

"There's no such thing as—wait, why does it complicate things?"

"Well, a warlock is like the advance scout for witches. He goes out and finds good locations with lots of kids for them to feast on." He nodded at me. "Obviously, he found one. So now we need to stop him before the rest of the coven gets here."

"Did you get a good look at that guy? Does he look dangerous to you? He's not a warlock. He's a nerd. He's probably, like, a teacher or something."

"That's what they want you to think. The least suspicious ones are usually the worst." He pointed toward the other room. "And that guy in there? He's probably the deadliest one of all."

I gulped and hated myself for it, because I'm pretty sure Tommy heard it too. If he thought I believed him about anything, he'd become relentless and impossible . . . well—even more impossible than usual. "Okay, I'm not saying I believe you, but . . . what do we do if he is a warlock?"

"Let me think." He pressed his fingers into his temples. It was his way of showing that he was thinking. He always did it, and it always annoyed me. "Okay, I think I have a plan."

I rolled my eyes. "Oh, that's a relief, because the last one you had worked so well."

"This is different," he said.

I knew it was going to be a mistake, but I asked anyway. "Okay, I know I'm going to regret this, but what's your plan?"

Tommy held his finger to his lips. "Shhhh! I don't want him to hear. Warlocks have super-sensitive hearing."

"You're thinking of dogs."

He ignored me again and placed his hand on my shoulder. "Don't worry, I'm not going to let what happened to Billy Thompson happen to my cousin."

"There was no Billy Thompson. You made him up."

"You don't have to pretend to be brave in front of me, okay?"

"But—"

He pinched his fingers together in front of my face. "Shhh! Just relax. Now, I need you to remember at dinner, you just follow my lead and do whatever I do, okay?"

Before I could answer, a shadow crossed our faces. We turned to see Herb standing in the doorway.

"Oh, I'm sorry to interrupt you, boys, but I seem to have misplaced my hat and I was wondering if I left it out here." He strolled into the room and eyed us before looking around.

"Uh, you weren't wearing a hat," I said.

"I wasn't?" He slapped his forehead. "Silly Herb. I am such a coo-coo-brain." He pushed his glasses up again. "Sometimes, I think I'd lose my head if it wasn't attached. Heh, heh." He took a few steps toward the other room and stopped in the doorway. "Oh, by the way, boys?" We both looked up. He looked back at us over his shoulder and grinned. "A mirror is for vampires."

He laughed and disappeared into the other room.

CHAPTER FOUR

DINNER AND A SHOW

If anybody had been watching that dinner, it would have looked like any other routine meal. I'd be saying that too if it wasn't happening to me. What those other people wouldn't have known was that at that moment, we were all in mortal danger of being instantly incinerated by a balding, glasses-wearing warlock by the name of Herbert Dorfman.

Okay, you have to trust me that it was a lot scarier than it sounded.

What made matters worse, was that at our nice big rectangular table, Herb was sitting at one end while Tommy insisted that we sit on either side of him. It was all part of his plan, he said. A plan which he had yet to reveal to me. I only hoped it was better than his brilliant mirror scheme.

Abby was on the same side as me, while Mom was on the same side as Tommy, with Dad all the way at the other end. If Herb had tried anything, by the time Dad got to us, we would've been mindless, demon, zombie-slaves in Herb's evil army.

Still, to be fair, I had to admit that Herb hadn't done anything strange as of yet. I only wish I could have said the same about Tommy.

Tommy had his own agenda and the scary thing was, I had absolutely no clue what he was planning, but by the way he kept nodding over to me, I had a horrible feeling that he thought I did.

Mom lifted a platter and offered it to Herb. "Chicken?"

"Oh, I'd love some." He took the platter from her and frowned before patting the table on both sides of his plate. "I'm sorry, but I don't seem to have any silverware."

Mom turned to Dad. "You didn't put out silverware?"

Dad's face fell. "I did," he said. "Uh, at least I thought I did. I don't know what happened to it."

"Oh, I have an extra fork by my plate, Aunt Megan." Tommy pointed over at me. "And I think Devin has an extra knife over there."

"Thank you, Tommy," Mom said.

"No problem."

I had no idea what Tommy was doing, but I rarely did. He nodded. I put my hands out to the side and shrugged.

He motioned toward Herb. "The knife. Give Herb the knife."

I rolled my eyes. He had the worst plans. I picked up the knife and extended it to Herb.

"And there!" Tommy said. He crossed the fork over the knife and held it in front of Herb.

I winced. Oh, no. I didn't even want to peek over at Mom. It couldn't be good.

Herb looked back and forth between Tommy and me. "Well, thank you . . . I guess." He reached out slowly, kind of inching his hand forward, paused a second, letting his hand linger over the crossed utensils, before finally snatching them up. "Much better now!" He smiled at us.

My shoulders sagged. So much for that.

I glanced over at Mom and immediately wished I hadn't.

Her mouth formed a thin line across her face. Her nostrils flared. She alternated glares between Tommy and me. "I apologize, Herb. I don't know what's gotten into them, they're usually not like this."

Dad arched an eyebrow. "They're not?"

"Oh," Herb laughed. "Not a problem at all. Boys will be boys, right? Why, back in my day, I was quite the rapscallion also."

"What?" I asked.

"Why, I remember this one time, I called up a neighbor and asked if her refrigerator was running." Herb kept laughing. "Well, when she answered yes, I said, well, you better go catch it." He dabbed at his eyes. "I guess you could tell, I was a lot wilder back then."

"Yeah, you were out of control," I said under my breath.

Mom clenched her fist so hard her knuckles turned white.

Herb caught it and turned to Mom. "Oh, I hope I didn't overstep my bounds and put any ideas in their heads. I know children are very impressionable at this age." He turned back to me. "Remember, kids, don't do any of the things that I did. It was a different time back then."

"I think they'll be okay," Dad said. "They're used to hearing some pretty crazy stories. Why, when I was designing the water recycling system at the mall, some of the things we did were hysterical. Like this one time, to test it out, we put this goldfish in the fountain and before you know it, that poor thing was sucked up into the system and . . ."

Great. The water recycling story again. I'd almost rather face the warlock. I needed to stop this now. "Mom, I'm hungry."

"Oh, that's right, where are my manners?" Mom pointed to the food on the table. "Please, everyone help yourselves."

Dad frowned and tried to continue the story, but when everyone concentrated on the food instead of him, he eventually gave up and stopped speaking.

I felt bad for a moment, but knew that if I didn't stop him, he'd go on telling recycling stories all night.

Everybody dug in and began serving themselves from the dishes laid out on the table. I just put food on my plate and kind of moved it around. I wasn't hungry. Couldn't really focus on it. Not when he was so close. Nobody else seemed to have any problems, though, and the next few moments were filled with the sounds of silverware scraping against dishes, until Mom spoke up.

"So, where do you come from, Herb?" Mom asked.

"Salem?" Tommy asked.

Herb shook his head. "Oh, no sir. I've never been to Massachusetts, although I'd love to go one day. I'm from Minnesota. We're the Gopher State."

"Gopher?" Abby shrieked. "The FAB used to have a gopher!" She turned to Dad. "I want a FAB! Not the gopher though, they're lame. I want the Cuddle Bunny."

"Now, sweetie," Dad said.

"The Cuddle Bunny is the best. I don't have one now, but I know Santa's going to bring me one for Christmas."

"Abby," Mom said.

"You like the FAB?" Herb asked.

Abby gasped. "You know what a FAB is?"

Herb smiled. "Maybe a little. Tell me what you think about it."

"The FAB is the best toy EVER!" Abby squealed. "It's a Furry Animated Bestie and they're amazing! They sing, they dance and everyone has one but me!" She pouted. I knew it was a show, but had to admit she was really good at it. "It's sooooo unfair!"

"Now, sweetie," Dad said. "They don't have any in the stores right now, remember?"

"All of my friends have a FAB. Like, every single one." She started counting off on her fingers. "Maya has one. Shaylee has one. Summer has one. Savanah has one."

"Abby," Mom said.

"The twins, Emily and Bianca, both have one."

"And Vanessa, Samantha, Destiny and Rebekah."

"Abby."

"And Steph. And Olivia. And Kiki. And—"

"Abby, I got it!" Mom snapped. "I told you, maybe Santa will bring you one."

"I'm pretty sure she's on Santa's other list," I said.

"Mom!"

"Devin!"

"Dad?" I said.

Dad looked at Mom and then hunched over his plate and scooped a spoon of rice into his mouth. He pointed to himself. "Eating," he mumbled through a full mouth.

"So, everyone has one of these FABs, you say?" Herb's eyes magnified behind his glasses.

She nodded. "Everyone but me."

Herb jabbed his finger in the air toward her. "Well, seems to me like you should have one too, young lady."

Abby clapped her hands so fast, they blurred in front of her face. "I should?"

Herb nodded. "Abso-tively!"

"Herb," Dad said. "Maybe you didn't hear the part about them not being available in any stores right now?"

Herb leaned in Abby's direction. "Sometimes, you just need to have some faith . . . and maybe . . ." He winked. "A little magic."

"Did you say magic?" Tommy asked.

"Oh, you betcha," he said. "Who doesn't love magic?"

I shrank back in my seat. "Do you do magic?"

Herb shrugged. "Oh, no. I mean, don't get me wrong. Sure, I like to dabble, but I'm no Doug Henning or anything."

"Who?" I asked.

"Could you do a trick?" Abby pleaded.

"Oh, I shouldn't." Herb waved his hands in front of him.

"Pleeeeaaaaaaase?" Abby wailed.

"Well, I suppose I could do one." Herb chuckled. "Very well. This is my famous levitating fork trick." He placed a napkin over his fork and began moving his hands in circles above it. "Abracadabra, Alakasable, make this fork rise above the table." He stopped waving his hands and shot his fingers out toward the fork.

The napkin twitched and shook.

My eyes widened.

Abby gasped.

The napkin slowly rose a couple of inches above the table.

Tommy and I glanced at each other.

I examined the floating napkin. There were no strings that I could make out. *How was he doing that?* I reached out for it, and it crashed down to the table with a clank.

Everybody burst into applause.

"Herb, that was amazing!" Mom said.

He waved his hand at her. "Oh, it was nothing. Just a little trick I learned many years ago."

I picked up the fallen fork and turned it over in my hands several times. "How'd you do that?"

Herb reached out and took the fork back from me. "A magician never reveals his secrets."

"Why do you have so many brooms?" Tommy blurted.

"Tommy!" Mom scolded. She turned to Herb. "I'm so sorry, Herb. I honestly don't know what's gotten into them today. I think maybe the excitement of meeting a new neighbor."

"Oh, no worries at all. They can ask me anything. I'm an open book. No secrets between good neighbors, I always say. But to answer your question, I keep a broom in every room of my house. You can never be too clean as far as I'm concerned."

"I wish the kids felt the same way about their rooms," Dad chimed in.

"Any other questions?" Herb asked.

Mom shook her head. "No, I'm sure they don't have—"

"Are you a cook?" I asked.

"Excuse me?" Herb said.

Tommy interrupted. "We saw them carry this huge pot into your house."

"Oh, that." He laughed again. "Well, I'm no Julia Child, but I like to fancy myself something of an amateur chef."

I looked over to Mom for help. "Who?"

"That pot is actually from a tribe in Papua, New Guinea," Herb continued. "You might say that I'm a collector of anything and everything. As a matter of fact, I have artifacts from all over the world. I'd be pleased to show them to you kids one day, if it's okay with your parents, that is."

I shook my head. "No."

"Oh, that sounds incredible," Mom cut in. "I'm sure they'd love to see. I would too actually."

"Fabulous!" Herb said. "We'll have to plan it."

Tommy looked at me and nodded. He tapped the table and mouthed the word "Now."

I shrugged and mouthed back "What?" but it was no use. He'd stopped paying attention to me. I had a very bad feeling.

Tommy swung his arm toward his glass of water, which he had placed along the edge of the table. "Oops!" It toppled over and spilled right onto Herb's lap.

"Tommy!" Mom said.

Herb jumped up. The bottom of his shirt and front of his pants were soaked.

Mom and Dad bolted to their feet.

My jaw dropped. I looked over at Tommy, but he just shrugged.

Mom covered her mouth for a moment. "I'm so sorry, Herb. I don't know what's going on, but I can't apologize enough."

Herb held his hands in front of him. "Please don't worry about it another second. Accidents happen. That's why they're called accidents." He chuckled. "Anyhoo, I should probably get going anyway. It's late and besides that, I'm tired from the move."

"Okay," Mom said. "But I'm sorry again."

"I'll walk you out," Dad said.

Herb gave a slight bow. "Thank you again for inviting a weary stranger into your home and making me feel welcome."

"Please know that you're welcome anytime," Mom said.

"Thank you. I'll be sure to take you up on that. I'm sure we'll be seeing a lot more of each other anyway." He glanced over to me. "And don't forget, when I'm all settled in, I'm going to have all of you over for dinner." He smiled. "I insist."

I watched as Dad walked Herb out of the room, with Abby running at their heels like a puppy. I picked up the fork again and examined it closely. Herb could say what he wanted, but I had been sitting closest to him. That fork floated for real.

Unfortunately, then came the bad part . . . Mom.

I don't even remember half the things she yelled at us about after that, because I was too busy thinking about dinner.

As much as I hated to admit it, there was no doubt in my mind anymore. Tommy was right.

I was living across the street from a warlock.

I'd been lying in my bed in the dark for I don't know how long without being able to fall asleep. It was a combination of reasons, really. First, there was the thought of a possible warlock living across the street. I knew there was no proof, but there was something about this guy, something weird.

Speaking of weird, that was the other thing keeping me up. As far as weird went, there was nobody weirder than the person pacing back and forth in my room for all that time: Tommy.

Every single time he comes for dinner, he somehow manages to get himself invited to sleep over. I'd have to speak to Mom about that.

"I can't see anything," Tommy said. "Maybe you could sneak into your mom's room and get my binoculars back?"

"Will you stop? She already thinks I'm a Peeping Tom because of you! I'm not doing it. And another thing, what were you doing at dinner? You made us look stupid."

"What are you talking about?"

"*What do I mean?* That stuff you were doing with the silverware!"

"What do you think I was doing? We made it into a cross." He thought a second. "Actually, I'm still not sure why it didn't work."

"*Why?*" I laughed. "Because it was only a knife and a fork that we just put across each other!"

"Exactly!" He snapped his fingers and pointed at me. "You just said it yourself. A cross."

"I said across. One word. Across. And it was more like an 'x' than a cross."

"A cross and an 'x' are pretty much the same thing."

I threw my hands up. "No, they're not! They're not the same thing at all."

"Hmmm, kind of are."

"No, they aren't. And besides, it was silverware! It wasn't going to do anything even if it was a cross!"

"Which it was."

I sighed. "And the water? That was your whole plan? To spill water on him?"

"I didn't see you come up with anything," he said. "And besides, I thought he would start melting. Witches melt from water."

"Says who?"

"Seriously? Didn't you ever watch *The Wizard of Oz*?"

"That was just a movie!"

"Where do you think they got it from? They did a lot of research before including it in the movie. Everybody knows that."

"Which comic book did you read that in?"

"FYI, most of the comics I read are based on fact and they all say water can melt witches."

"I don't believe that part. And even it was true, don't you think that it would probably have to be holy water like you said?"

"Duh, do you think I'm stupid?"

"Yes."

He ignored me. "I blessed it first."

That did it. "That doesn't even make any sense. You're not a priest. It can't be real holy water without a priest blessing it."

"Well, I didn't have time to go to a priest, did I?"

"Then, moron, it wouldn't work. How did you bless it?"

"Well, I wasn't exactly sure what the right blessing was, so I just said grace."

I let out a long stream of air. "Uh-huh. And how will that help exactly?"

He crossed the room and stood by my window. "With these things, it's the intent that matters. Like if you think about it and believe, it counts."

"This isn't like 'clap if you believe in fairies' stuff. It doesn't work that way."

"Uh-oh." Tommy got quiet.

I didn't like the sound of that. "What? What's wrong?" I said.

He motioned me over. "Come take a look at this."

I slid out of my bed and across Tommy's sleeping bag on the floor until I reached the window. It was dark out, but a lamppost allowed us to see a little. We craned our necks to see around the tree to get a better glimpse of Herb's house.

"What am I looking at?" I asked.

He held up his hand. "Wait for it."

After a few moments of darkness, one of the windows flared up with a burst of colors coming from inside. Red, green, yellow, and purple flashed from within before settling back into darkness again.

"Something's going on inside over there."

My heart started to pound. "What do you think it is?"

He shrugged. "I don't know, but we need to check it out."

"What? Us? Why?"

"Because if it's happening, we need proof. The sooner we find out what that warlock is up to, the sooner we can show everyone and make plans to stop him. Otherwise, you'll be just another victim like Billy Thompson."

"You made him up."

"We don't have time for that!" He pointed at the window. "We have to go out there right now and see what he's doing."

My mouth went dry. "Now?" I stared out the window and saw how dark it was. "I don't think it's a good idea to go out there at this time of night. I-i-it's late and my parents would kill me." A numbness went through my body. "He's probably just watching TV or something." A small boom, like thunder, cracked outside. "What was that?"

Lightning blazed across the sky, lighting everything in its path, until it struck Herb's roof. The house lit up for a moment like fireworks on the Fourth of July. Soon after, smoke seeped out the window and drifted into the night.

Tommy turned to me. "That's not the TV."

CHAPTER FIVE

THERE'S A LIGHT OVER AT THE DORFMAN PLACE

Don't look down. That's what I kept thinking. It was a lot higher than it looked from inside my bedroom. One slip and I'd fall to the ground and maybe break my neck and die. The longer I thought about it, the more I realized what a stupid idea this was. I was an absolute idiot to let Tommy talk me into crawling out my window in the middle of the night and onto the tree branch. *Why did I keep listening to him?*

My hands trembled too much to fully concentrate. Each time the branch swayed, my heart went with it. I wanted to throw up, except I was worried that if I did, I might lose my hold and fall to the ground. Bottom line? I wanted to be anywhere else but here.

I was breathing fast and heavy. "I can't do it," I said. "We have to turn around now and go back inside. We're going to die."

"Stop being a drama queen. We're not going to die. At the most, maybe we'll break a few bones or something."

I made the mistake of peeking down. "Please, let's turn around and go back. I'm begging you."

"We're already too far out, keep going."

The night air was cold, and the breeze made it feel even colder going through the thin fabric of my sweatpants. This was no way to dress for a winter night.

"It's freezing out here," I said. "It feels like Alaska."

"You don't know that. You've never been to Alaska."

"It's an expression."

"Just keep going."

The leaves rustled all around. The shadows wouldn't let me see past what was immediately in front of me. I kept expecting something to jump out at us. That's all I needed, for some squirrel to attack and chew my face off. I was going to kill Tommy. "This is so bad. We should've just gone out the front door, like I said."

"We've been over this a thousand times already, you know your parents would've heard us leave your room. This is the best way, trust me."

I'd heard him say that line many times before. Unfortunately, I usually did whatever he asked. Almost every time. Mom said I was too much of a follower with him, and in the back of my mind, I knew she was right. Tommy would say something, it made sense at the time, and I would do it. I'd always seem to regret it minutes later. Hopefully, this time, I wouldn't die because of it.

I closed my eyes as I hugged the branch, inching along, trying to reach the main part of the tree. *Don't look down. Don't look down.* Then I heard something. Like a purring maybe, but not exactly. I lifted my head and opened my eyes to come face to face with two large, bright-yellow eyes.

An owl.

"Whoo?" the owl hooted.

It was the size of a baby elephant. Okay, I'm exaggerating. In reality, it was probably no bigger than a small dog, but in my mind, it seemed humongous. So, under the circumstances, I did the only thing I could think of. I panicked.

I started sliding back along the branch toward the window. "Tommy!" I backed into him.

"What are you doing?" he said.

The owl took a couple of hops toward me and twisted its neck to the side, looking grotesquely like its head was about to snap off.

"It's an owl!" I said.

"Shhh!" Tommy said. "It knows it's an owl. Now be quiet, you're going to wake the whole neighborhood. Keep going."

"Are you kidding me?" The owl was less than a foot away. It blinked a couple of times, but never took its eyes off of me. I glanced back at Tommy and shook my head. "No!"

The branch started to curve downward a little. I hugged it tighter.

"Go!" Tommy said. "This branch isn't strong enough to hold both of us if our weight is in the same spot. Keep going! He's more scared of you than you are of him!"

I flinched as the owl took another hop toward me. "Trust me, he's not!"

The branch bent some more and we started sliding downward.

Tommy pushed me. "Go!"

I swatted behind me, hoping to hit him. "No! Go back to the house."

"The branch is already lower than the window! Keep going!"

A sharp, biting pain. "Ow!" I turned to see the owl's beak clamped down on my finger. I tried swatting at him, but he just flapped his wings some while still holding on.

Creeeeeeak! The branch tilted some more, groaning under our weight.

"Move!" Tommy said.

"I can't!" I gripped tighter. So did the owl. I wanted to scream, but couldn't take the chance of waking Mom and Dad. Blood started trickling out, staining my finger and making my hold on the branch slippery, loosening my grip.

"Get out of the way," Tommy said. "I'll get rid of that stupid owl."

"Where do you want me to go?"

The owl released its hold and started pecking at my hand. I jumped back more.

"Noooo!" Tommy said. "Go back up! It's not going to hol—"

SNAP!

I had just enough time to see the owl flap away before the branch broke and we fell.

In case you're wondering, the answer is seven. Seven branches between us and the ground. I know, because we hit every single one of them before we landed with a thud.

I groaned. "Oof!"

I eased my arms up and wiggled my fingers. I winced as I bent each knee to check my legs. Other than the almost intolerable pain everywhere, I was mostly okay. I stared up at the tree above us and looked past it to the stars. There was something almost peaceful about it. Even with all the aches, I wanted to fall asleep right there, on the grass of my front yard, until all that beauty and serenity was eclipsed by one large, ugly face . . . Tommy's.

He stared down at me. "Hey, lucky for us all those branches broke our fall, huh?"

Ignoring the pain, I shot my arms up and grabbed him by the throat. I was up in a flash and pounced on him, hitting him with one strike after another. "I hate you. I hate you. I hate you!"

He held his hands up, trying to block me. "Ow, what are you doing?"

I continued hitting him. "This is all your fault. You and your stupid ideas. Going out my window in the middle of the night. We could've been killed!"

"But we weren't!"

"But we could've been."

"But we weren't." Tommy grabbed my wrists. "Stop hitting me and listen for a second!"

"What?"

"First of all, get off of me, you're heavy."

I stared at him a moment, deciding whether or not to hit him at least once more, but I finally rolled off. "Fine. What else?"

"I'm sorry about the tree, but we were really lucky."

"You better have more to say than that," I said.

"Okay, but how was I supposed to know there'd be a stupid owl there? The important thing is that we're down. Now let's use this as our opportunity to go spy on Herb."

I glanced across the street and then back up to my window. "I *really* think we should go back into the house."

"And how do you want to do that?" Tommy pointed up. "There's nothing to climb back up on anymore."

I looked up and realized that all that empty sky I had just been staring at used to be filled with the branches close to my window. "I'm so dead," I said.

He waved his hand from side to side. "Our way back in is lying all over your yard now."

I put my hands on top of my head. "They're going to kill me."

He shook his head. "Don't worry. I'll figure something out. Your mom loves me." He got to his feet and started walking across the yard.

"Where are you going?" I called.

He looked over his shoulder. "Weren't you listening? We're going to Herb's, where else?" He waved me over. "Now, c'mon."

I bolted to my feet and ran after him. "We can't still go to Herb's now! We have to go back inside. Seriously, you don't know my mom for real. She's nice to you because she's your aunt, so she has to be, but she's really going to kill me."

Tommy shrugged. "Maybe, but then what difference does it make if we go in now or later?"

"What?"

"I mean, if you already know they're going to kill you, it doesn't matter if we go in now or later. It's not like you're going to get into any more trouble by going to spy on Herb first, right? You'll still get into the same amount of trouble, so it just makes sense to do all you can before it happens."

"I guess, but—"

"Exactly. And maybe if we get some proof that he's a warlock, the whole town will thank us and we might even get a reward. Your mom and dad can't punish us if we're heroes."

I held my hands up. "Stop! Every time you say something, it confuses me, and then I'm the one who winds up getting in trouble."

"You won't get in trouble for this. Well, not in any more trouble than you're already in. So, c'mon." He started walking again.

I watched him walk and sighed. Tommy always seemed so confident and acted like he knew what he was doing. The exact opposite of me. Even now, I had to admit that a part of me was glad he was taking the lead on this, since I had absolutely no idea what to do. I did what I usually did with him: followed.

Everything was silent. No cars or people out at all. That was one of the drawbacks of living on a quiet street. Nobody around to help when an evil warlock might be on the prowl.

I shivered as the wind cut right through my sweatpants and T-shirt. I wished I'd thought to put on a jacket before we left.

We crossed the street to Herb's house.

Tall hedges surrounded his property. I realized the window we had seen easily from my second-floor room was much more difficult to make out from the ground and was blocked by hedges. We would have to go through them if we wanted to get there, which meant we would be on his property and blocked from anyone else being able to see us.

"I don't think this is such a good idea," I whispered.

"Relax," Tommy said. "You worry too much. Trust me."

"You keep saying that and I don't."

He ignored me and shoved some of the hedges aside and slunk through.

I didn't want to follow him inside. Every voice in my head was screaming at me not to, but I wanted even less to be left alone without him. Again, I followed.

After a few steps, Tommy turned to me. "See? Nothing to worry about."

I wished for once I could be like him. Not scared all the time.

We crept toward the window where we had seen all the lights. Tommy held his finger to his lips.

My heart was going like a machine-gun. I needed to breathe, calm down.

We lifted our heads a little at a time and peered in through the glass.

It was a large room with a fire blazing inside a humongous fireplace. Also in the fireplace, the cauldron. And in front of the cauldron, Herb.

And he didn't look happy.

The sounds coming from inside were muffled because of the closed window, but we were still able to hear bits and pieces.

"Work already!" Herb yelled.

He kicked the cauldron and immediately winced. His face went red as he grabbed his foot and hopped around.

Tommy and I glanced at each other.

"You sure this guy is a warlock?" I asked.

Tommy nodded. "Trust me, they're sneaky. He may already know we're here. Just be alert."

Herb rubbed his toes and then paced the room, back and forth, again and again, every so often stopping in front of the cauldron and pulling at the few wisps of hair that he had left. "Think, Herb! Think!" He did this several times, until he finally stopped. His eyes widened. He ran to the side of the room, out of our line of vision.

We craned our necks to try to see, but couldn't make out anything.

"What's he doing?" I whispered.

Tommy shrugged. "Maybe looking into his crystal ball to spy on us. We might be compromised."

"Stop with that word!"

Herb came back into view, carrying a vial of some sort of red liquid.

"What is that?" I asked.

"If I had to guess," Tommy said. "I'd say human blood."

"No, it's not."

"Shhh!"

Herb approached the cauldron and reached up to the mantle over the fireplace and lifted . . . a wand.

Tommy gave me one of his I-told-you-so smirks.

Herb said something, but I couldn't make it out. He tapped the vial three times and poured it into the cauldron. It erupted instantly, shooting flames upward like a spewing volcano. I could even hear the roar from outside. It lasted a few seconds and then subsided back into the pot, but an eerie reddish glow remained, lighting up the room.

Herb dipped the vial back into the cauldron and scooped out a sample. He held it up in front of him. It reflected off his glasses, obscuring his eyes. He dipped the wand into the vial and brought it back out. I wasn't sure what was brighter now, the wand or Herb's smile.

He walked back to the side and stopped. It was right where he had disappeared before, but this time he wasn't completely out of view. I was still able to see most of him. He waved the wand in a circle several times while saying something, and then thrust his hand forward. A flash of light.

Herb leaned in. He didn't move, just stared at whatever it was he was looking at. Slowly, he drew his hands back and thrust his arms into the air, pumping them up and down several times, looking like a gunfighter who had just won a duel. He laughed.

"What is he doing?" I asked.

Suddenly, a black cat jumped onto the sill and rammed against the window, hissing at us.

"Aaaaaaaagh!" We screamed at the same time.

Herb whipped his head in our direction. Our eyes locked.

"Get down!" I said.

Tommy and I fell back, but it was too late. Herb had seen us.

"Run!" Tommy said.

We scrambled through the hedges and bolted like lightning across the street. The sound of our feet echoed through the neighborhood. We reached my yard. Tommy tripped on one of the branches that had snapped off. I couldn't avoid him and went tumbling over him. Both of us went sprawling.

"What are you doing?" I said. "Get up!"

"What do you want from me?" Tommy said. "I tripped!"

"Get up!" I staggered to my feet and ran up the porch and pounded on the door.

"MOM! DAD! Open up!"

We heaved ourselves at the door, ramming our sides into it, again and again. *Please open up!* I pictured Mom and Dad's faces, seeing two piles of ashes on the ground by the time they got to us.

"Hurry!" I said.

Finally, the door flew open, sending Tommy and me crashing to the floor in a heap.

Mom stood over us, her eyes blazing. "What is going on? Why are you outside?"

I jumped to my feet. "No time now!" I grabbed the door and slammed it shut, but not before I saw something out of the corner of my eye. Something sitting on the porch, glaring at us.

Something small, black, and furry.

CHAPTER SIX

NEVER ACCEPT GIFTS FROM STRANGERS OR WARLOCKS

I spent the better part of two hours listening to Mom yell. She'd made a checklist of all the things I'd done wrong and tacked a punishment on to each one. According to my calculations, I was grounded until sometime after my 102nd birthday.

That actually didn't bother me as much as her sending Tommy home first thing in the morning. Normally I would've been fine with it, but as much as I hated to admit it, I wished he were still there.

Sure, he was annoying. Sure, he got on my nerves. And sure, he had absolutely no idea what he was talking about. But still, the good thing about Tommy was that he thought he did, and right now, I kind of needed that.

Without him there, I hadn't left my room. I tried to keep an eye on Herb as best as I could, but hadn't seen him leave his house. I'm not sure what I was expecting to see anyway, but it sure would be nice to catch him doing something. Not that anybody would ever believe me. The guy looked more like an insurance salesman than a dangerous warlock, but that didn't matter. I had to find out for myself. I got out of bed to take yet one more look out the window, and I saw him.

Herb! And he was walking away from my house!

I leaned against the window, pressing my hands and face to the glass. My heart thumped wildly. What was he up to?

He crossed the street back to his home, and I heard what was quite possibly the loudest noise ever in the history of the universe.

"*Mooooooooooooooommm!*"

It was Abby. Herb must've done something to her!

I bolted from my room and rushed down the stairs, two at a time, toward the sound. I skidded to a stop in the living room.

Mom and Dad were already there.

Abby was dancing and twirling around. She was holding something.

I walked closer and there it was. The realization of it smacked me in the face. Abby had in her arms one white-furred, floppy-eared Cuddle Bunny. It had large, oval, black button eyes, with a little strip of brown fur at the top for eyelids. Long whiskers extended from each side.

Abby shrieked. *"I GOT A CUDDLE BUNNEEEEEEE!"*

Mom turned to Dad. "You got her a Cuddle Bunny? They can't be found anywhere. How did you get one? How much did you spend?"

Dad shook his head so fast, it looked like he was watching a high-speed tennis match. "No, I promise! It was on the porch in a box."

"What?" Tingling went up my back, like thousands of tiny spiders crawling at once. A cold feeling washed over me.

"Then who would get her a Cuddle Bunny?" Mom asked.

"Santa did!" Abby said. "Just like you said he would, because I've been soooooo good!"

"I'm not really sure you know what the word 'good' means," I said.

"Mom!"

"Devin!"

"Dad," I said.

Dad held his hand up. "Uh, one second, let me just take a look and see if there's a note or something." He grabbed the box the Cuddle Bunny had come in and turned it over. A small yellow Post-it fluttered to the floor.

Mom walked over and picked it up. "It's from Herb."

"Herb?" I leaped across the room, snatched the Cuddle Bunny from Abby, and held it by the ears at arm's length. "You have to get rid of it! It's evil! Send it back. Wait! I'll stuff it down the garbage disposal."

"What are you doing?" Mom asked.

Abby tried to grab it back, but I kept it away from her.

"GIVE. ME. MY. CUDDLE BUNNY!"

"No!" I shouted. "It's too dangerous, we have to destroy this thing!"

"Mom!" Abby ran in place, alternating stomping each foot down.

"Devin, give it to her now!" Mom said.

"But Mom, Herb is an evil warlock and this is his plan to murder us all!"

"What are you talking about?" Mom's face scrunched up. "A warlock?"

I nodded. "Yes."

"And he's going to kill us with a Cuddle Bunny?" Dad asked.

"Yes!"

"Uh-huh," Dad said. "Devin, could you do me a favor and just take a look at the Cuddle Bunny?"

"Dad, you have to—"

"Just one look, Devin."

"But—"

"Look."

I stared at the lifeless Cuddle Bunny in my hands. It sort of hung to the side, with its large button eyes staring back at me, unmoving. From the outside, it looked just like any other stuffed animal, but I knew it wasn't. "Okay, I know what it looks like, but—"

"No buts!" Mom said. "Now, stop being ridiculous and give her the Cuddle Bunny back!"

My shoulders slumped and my head drooped as I handed the Cuddle Bunny to Abby.

She glared at me as she snatched it away and clutched it to her chest. "Are you okay, little bunny?"

Mom sighed. "May I read the note now?"

I looked away and nodded.

"Good," she continued. "It says, *Just a little token of my appreciation for a fabulous dinner and inviting a grateful neighbor into your home.*" She turned to Dad. "That's so sweet of him."

"We can't keep it," I said.

Dad snorted. "They're going for around three hundred dollars on eBay right now. Of course we can keep it."

Abby squeezed the Cuddle Bunny. "I have a Cuddle Bunny! I can't believe I finally have a Cuddle Bunny. I waited forever and ever and ever without one." Her eyes narrowed. "I can't wait to call Emma. She thinks she's so special because she got a Hugging Hippo, but wait 'til she hears that I got a Cuddle Bunny."

"I thought you said all your friends had a Cuddle Bunny," Mom said.

"Not Emma. She got a Hugging Hippo and they're stupid." She turned back to the Cuddle Bunny. "Your ear is bent, little bunny." She stared at it a second and then a wide smile brightened her face. "I'm going to name you Mr. Flopsy-Ears."

"Awww," Mom said. "That's such a cute name."

"And in today's news, Mr. Flopsy-Ears murders a family in their sleep," I said.

"Devin," Mom said through gritted teeth. "That's enough."

I stared into her eyes and saw she had the "Mom-look-of-no-back-talk" on. I zipped my lips. No sense in arguing now, especially with the Cuddle Bunny just hanging limp in Abby's arms. I'm not sure I'd believe me either.

Abby held the Cuddle Bunny up in front of her. "I love you, Mr. Flopsy-Ears." She frowned. "Mom, it's not doing anything!" She shook the Cuddle Bunny. "*Why isn't my Cuddle Bunny doing anything?*"

"I think it needs batteries," Dad said. "I have some in the fridge."

"Oh yeah!" Abby squeezed the Cuddle Bunny again. "Does Mr. Flopsy-Ears need batteries? Come on, let's get you some."

As she ran off, I did a double take. Was it my imagination, or did Mr. Flopsy-Ears just wink at me?

CHAPTER SEVEN

BE VERY, VERY QUIET, I'M HUNTING ~~RABBITS~~ BUNNIES

I spent the next couple of days stalking Abby, following her everywhere, with very little result.

That didn't mean that I wasn't going to try. Abby and Mr. Flopsy-Ears weren't going to make a move without me tailing them. Abby went to the living room, and I'd go too. Abby went to the kitchen, and I'd suddenly want a snack. If Abby went out in the yard, I'd need a breath of fresh air. Any move she'd make, I'd be there. The problem was that so far, I hadn't seen a thing, but I knew that didn't mean there was nothing there to see.

Sure, there were a few times where I could have sworn I saw a blink or a twitch, but nothing for sure. I couldn't push this yet, not without proof. Mom and Dad already thought

I was crazy because of the warlock talk, so I needed something to show them that I wasn't.

The only place I hadn't been able to follow was her room, since she shut the door behind her, but that didn't stop me from trying. Yeah, I felt a little stupid listening to her door, but I knew it was for her own protection.

After making sure nobody was coming, I pressed my ear to the door.

That's when I quickly realized that there was something I'd forgotten about the Cuddle Bunny.

The song.

That stupid, annoying song. The chorus, to be exact. That horrible, awful chorus that Abby would play over and over and over again.

I'm your furry bestie
Never need to test me
Because one thing will always be true
No matter where you go, I will find you.

I don't even know how many verses there were in total. She never got far enough to finish. It was always chorus and replay, chorus and replay. That chorus wormed its way into your ear and ate away at your brain. You just had to hope that it didn't get to you, because if it did, you'd become one of the countless, mindless zombie hordes at the mercy of the FAB.

So, bottom line? I needed to get rid of the Cuddle Bunny, which wasn't going to be easy with Abby taking Mr. Flopsy-Ears with her almost everywhere she went.

If there was ever a time that she didn't have the Cuddle Bunny with her, I'd missed it. Either it didn't happen, or I had horrible timing catching it . . . until now.

"Abby!" It was Mom.

Uh-oh. There was absolutely no place to hide in the hallway. I scanned the area fast and bolted into my room just as Abby opened her door.

"What, Mom?" Abby asked.

I gently nudged my door almost all the way closed and hid behind it, so Abby wouldn't see me.

"Time for your shower," Mom said.

"Aww!" Abby said. "Do I have to? I want to play with Mr. Flopsy-Ears."

"You can play with Mr. Flopsy-Ears later. Shower now!"

I imagined Abby's face and wished I could see it. Usually, when she was forced to do something she didn't want, her eyes turned into lasers and she would incinerate anyone in her line of vision with her laser death stare. Okay, that last part wasn't true, but it was pretty close.

"Can I bring Mr. Flopsy-Ears?" Abby called out.

"No, I'm not taking a chance on the Cuddle Bunny getting wet. If it gets ruined, you'll never get another one. Just leave him on your bed and he'll be waiting for you when you get out."

"*Fine.*" I could hear the acid in her voice and loved every second of it.

Within minutes, I heard Abby bound down the hallway toward the bathroom.

I waited a moment until I was sure she was gone and peeked out into the hallway.

Clear.

I crept down the hall to Abby's room. Her door was open.

I spotted him immediately.

Mr. Flopsy-Ears was on her bed, just lying there.

I took a step in and stopped. My legs trembled and I felt stupid.

Mr. Flopsy-Ears hadn't moved.

I inched closer.

His black button eyes stared up at me.

I braced myself, in case he attacked.

Still nothing.

"You're not fooling anyone, you know," I said.

The Cuddle Bunny just stared.

"I know you winked before." I leaned closer and looked into its eyes. "Herb, if you're listening to this, you can forget about your evil plan. I'm onto you."

Still nothing.

"Okay, Mr. Flopsy-Ears. You listen and you listen good. I'm warning you, I'm keeping an eye on you. You're not going to get away with anything. You can think you're fooling Mom and Dad, but I'm going to be watching you *very* closely. And the second you mess up . . ." I jabbed my finger into his face. "You're finished."

Out of the corner of my eye, I saw movement by the doorway.

I whirled toward it to see Dad standing there.

His mouth was open. He glanced back and forth between me and Mr. Flopsy-Ears.

I tried to act naturally. "Oh, hey, Dad."

He pointed. "Were you just talking to the Cuddle Bunny?"

I turned to Mr. Flopsy-Ears. "This Cuddle Bunny?"

He looked around the room. "Do you see other Cuddle Bunnies?"

I also looked around the room. "No. Why, do you?"

"No." He paused. "But why are you talking to this Cuddle Bunny?"

I shrugged. "No reason."

Dad stared at me. "Uh-huh."

"They say you have to talk to them to get them to interact with you. That's how they work, you know."

"I know how they work. I'm not sure you're supposed to threaten them, though."

"I wanted it to work faster."

He stared at me for a few more seconds and sighed. "Okay, let's get out of here before Abby gets out of the shower. You know how angry she'll get if she finds you in her room."

I took one more look at Mr. Flopsy-Ears before I walked over to Dad.

Mr. Flopsy-Ears never moved.

73

That night I lay in bed for hours. I just couldn't fall asleep. I knew there was something wrong with that Cuddle Bunny, but really, what could I prove? After following Abby and Mr. Flopsy-Ears around for days, I had nothing. But I knew what I saw. I knew that Bunny was alive and up to no good. I needed proof, but had very little idea about how to get it.

Rain pelted the windows and thunder cracked outside. The noise did nothing to calm my nerves. Practically every sound made me jump. The booming across the sky. The pellets, like little bullets, bombarding my window. The little footsteps and the creaking of the floorboards in the hallway.

Wait.

Little footsteps?

I bolted upright in bed and listened.

More creaking.

My heart started to pound.

I wanted to call out, but that wouldn't do any good. It'd just warn Mr. Flopsy-Ears to go hide, and I needed to catch that little Bunny in the act.

I slipped out of bed, tiptoed across the room, and inched the door open. The hallway was dark, except for the occasional flash of lightning that streaked in through the blinds. It felt like my heart jumped into my throat and cut off all the air. I took a deep breath, trying to get air into my lungs, before I took a peek out.

Nothing.

My hands trembled.

74

C'mon, Devin, don't be scared now.

I stepped out and looked around. Everything on my body tingled. It was like when I slept on my arm and couldn't move it until the blood started to circulate again. Only this time, it was everywhere.

I didn't see anything and crept toward Abby's room.

CREAK!

The floorboards behind me!

I whirled toward the sound.

"Hello?" I said quietly.

A shadow scurried across the light of the blinds.

I jumped. *What was that?*

I swallowed hard. My breathing echoed throughout the hall, drowning out the noise from the thunderstorm.

Ahead of me, another creaking sound.

My legs wobbled.

Easy now. I took a deep breath and exhaled through my mouth.

Inhale. Relax. Exhale. Relax.

Inhale. Exhale. Inhale. Exhale.

I crept the rest of the way through the shadowy hallway until I got to Abby's room. I reached for the door, but yanked my arm back. It was already opened a crack.

I clenched and unclenched my fists. My palms were sweaty. I knew the door being open meant absolutely nothing, but my brain was screaming differently. My arm shook as I reached for the handle.

I nudged it and winced as it screeched. *Keep it quiet!* I peered in. Nothing looked out of place. I stepped a toe in her room, like I was testing water in a pool. I don't know what I was expecting to happen, but when nothing did, I stepped inside.

The thunder roared, and I flinched.

Steady, Devin. Steady!

I tiptoed to Abby's bed.

There she was, sound asleep. Her arms wrapped around the Cuddle Bunny. I puffed out a breath. I'd never been so relieved to see a stuffed animal. I was just imagining things. I took a few steps closer and cocked my head.

"What the—?"

In her arms, something white and smooth, but it wasn't a Cuddle Bunny!

A pillow!

More scurrying behind me. I whipped around.

BOOM! The thunder cracked.

The lightning flashed.

On the windowsill, smiling, its eyes narrowed.

The Cuddle Bunny! He pointed to himself and then put his paws up by his throat and pretended to choke himself until his head flopped to the side and then pointed at me. He pulled his paws away and smiled.

Acting on instinct, I did the first thing that popped into my head.

I screamed.

I backed into a dresser. My feet tangled with the leg. I stumbled and went down with a crash.

"*Mooooooooommm!*" Abby jumped up and screamed.

The sound of running footsteps outside the room.

The lights snapped on.

"Devin!" Mom's voice. "What are you doing in here?"

Mom and Dad each gripped one of my arms and yanked me to my feet.

I pointed to the window. "The Cuddle Bunny!"

Everyone looked.

The Cuddle Bunny wasn't there.

Dad tapped me on the shoulder and pointed to Abby's bed. "It's right there, Devin."

I turned toward Abby's bed and saw Mr. Flopsy-Ears in her arms. "But it was by the window just a second ago! I promise!"

Mom pressed her hand to my forehead. "Are you feeling okay?"

I pushed her arm away. "I'm not sick! I'm telling you, it was just standing right by the window. It smiled at me."

Dad scowled. "It smiled at you?"

I threw my hands up. "Yes! And also said he was going to strangle me."

Dad arched his eyebrow. "He said that?"

I thought a moment. "Well, not with words, but he held his paws to his throat and threatened me."

"Uh-huh," Dad said and glanced at Mom.

"Dad, you have to believe me! It's evil! Herb did something to it and it's going to kill us all."

Dad pointed to the lifeless toy. "That thing?"

"Don't let it fool you, Dad! It's bad. I mean, like really, really bad."

He walked over to it.

I reached out. "Don't!"

"It's okay, Devin." He petted the Cuddle Bunny in Abby's arms. "See, Devin." He sang the words. "I don't know what your obsession with the Cuddle Bunny is, but Mr. Flopsy-Ears is nice. He's not going to hurt anybody. There's nothing to be afraid of."

My chest heaved. I realized I was breathing hard. "It's only pretending, Dad. Don't fall for it."

Dad studied my face. I already saw that he didn't believe me.

Abby's eyes narrowed. Her bottom lip curled into a pout. She glared at me. "You leave Mr. Flopsy-Ears alone!"

"Abby, I'm trying to save you!" I said. "I don't want it to hurt you."

"Mom, Devin is scaring me." She hugged the Cuddle Bunny tight, jumped out of bed, and ran behind Mom.

"But—" I protested.

From behind Mom, the Cuddle Bunny stuck his tongue out at me.

I pointed. "There! *Did you see that?* He stuck his tongue out at me!"

Everyone turned to the Cuddle Bunny, but he looked normal again. Like any regular stuffed animal.

Mom and Dad glanced at each other.

Mom took a step toward me. "Devin . . ."

I moved to the side and wagged my finger at the Cuddle Bunny. "You won't get away with this, Mr. Flopsy-Ears. You're not fooling me. I know what you are."

Dad placed his hand on my shoulder. "Um, Devin? Why don't you go wait for me in your room? I'll be in in a second."

I gritted my teeth. "Fine, but you're going to be sorry you didn't listen to me."

Abby clutched the Cuddle Bunny to her chest. "I'm not going let mean Devin hurt you."

I stormed out of the room, thinking only one thing as I went.

Mr. Flopsy-Ears had to go.

CHAPTER EIGHT

THE BUBBLE BATTLE BRIGADE, OR TOMMY'S RIDICULOUS IDEA

The next day, I kept a constant vigil over Mr. Flopsy-Ears and followed Abby everywhere. But once again, he never did a thing. This time I wasn't buying it at all. I know what I saw. It came down to proof and I knew it. Without it, nobody would believe me. Already I had to bite my tongue and stop accusing the Cuddle Bunny of being alive and dangerous, especially with the way Mom and Dad kept whispering about me when they didn't think I could hear.

I had to catch that crazy little rabbit in the act, because whenever I wasn't near Abby, every little noise made me jump. Every tiny sound had me diving for cover. My nerves were frazzled. I couldn't go on like this. The Bunny had to go.

It took a while, but my chance finally came. Mom and Abby were going out shopping and I got to stay home with Dad, but between him playing his video games and taking his naps, he'd be easy to get around.

I had this planned well. First thing, I peeked through the living room window to watch Mom's car pull out of the driveway, keeping track of it until it disappeared down the street. I turned back into the room. Dad was already out of it, snoring on the couch. That was his usual routine whenever Mom left the house, but even for him, this was record time.

I glanced at the clock on the wall. Mom wouldn't be back for a while, but I couldn't waste any time either. This needed to be taken care of today, even if it meant resorting to desperate measures. I peered out the window once more, tiptoed across the room, and eased the door open. Fortunately, Tommy was already there, waiting.

Unfortunately, he was covered in bubble wrap and wearing a football helmet. He held a baseball bat with one hand and carried a large brown garbage bag with the other. I already regretted asking him to come.

"You rode all the way from your house dressed like that?"

"Danger doesn't take a break for fashion."

"Whatever. Come in." I grabbed him by the plastic around his chest, causing a couple of his bubbles to pop, and yanked him inside.

"Where is he?" Tommy asked.

81

I held my finger to my lips and motioned toward the couch, where Dad's snores sounded like a stable of grunting pigs.

Tommy nodded as we made our way to the staircase. He couldn't bend his knees from all the plastic wrapped around him, so he kind of had to swing his legs out to the side and teeter back and forth as he went.

"You look like a stupid penguin," I whispered.

"I don't care what I look like," he said. "I'm safer this way. Now, take this!" He handed me the bag.

"You rode with this all the way here?"

"It was murder." He motioned to the stairs. "Now, let's go."

We crept up the steps one at a time. I'm not sure Dad would've heard us over his snores, but if anything could have done it, it was the sound of Tommy's bubble-wrapped legs rubbing together.

"You might as well get a bullhorn and announce that we're coming."

"Trust me, nobody's hearing a thing over your dad's snores. It sounds like a buzzsaw every six seconds."

We reached the top and Tommy pointed to the bag. "Put it on."

"Are you sure this is necessary?" I asked.

Tommy nodded. "Trust me, I've seen this type of thing before."

"No you haven't."

"You don't know the things that I've seen. Anyway, you'll thank me for this later. Now, put it on!"

I sighed, turned over the bag, and dumped out the contents. A large tube of bubble wrap and a football helmet tumbled out.

"Seriously?"

He nodded. "Just do it."

I placed one end of the bubble wrap to my chest while Tommy took the other end and circled around me over and over until I was completely covered in plastic. I looked like a bubble-mummy, and I felt like a fool.

"And finally." He placed the football helmet on my head. "Okay, *now* you're ready for battle."

"Are you sure? Maybe a suit of armor too?"

"Ha ha. You won't be laughing when this saves your life. Now, let's do this."

I took a deep breath. "Okay, let's go."

We wobbled over to Abby's door. Tommy pressed his ear to it.

"What are you doing?" I whispered.

"I wanted to see if we could catch him in the act," Tommy said.

"The act of what?"

"Spying or sabotage or whatever else he's up to." Tommy listened for a moment more and nodded. "Okay, on the count of three we rush in and stick to the plan."

I turned to Tommy. "Plan?"

"One."

"Wait! What plan?"

"Two."

"You never said anything about a plan."

"Three!" Tommy flung the door open and wobbled in, the bat raised high above his head.

Before I could react, he brought the bat crashing down again and again. His swings were a blur and the loud thwacking sound of bat striking mattress echoed throughout the room.

I rushed to his side, making sure to avoid his swing. In my mind, I'd already started trying to come up with excuses for Mr. Flopsy-Ears' destruction. So far, I didn't have much, other than me saying Tommy had snapped and gone insane, which I had to admit didn't seem that far-fetched.

"Stop!" I said.

Tommy lowered the bat. His eyes were blazing. "*What?* You can't stop me in the middle!"

I examined the bed, hoping to find Cuddle Bunny carnage, but was disappointed to see that Tommy had been striking nothing but—"A pillow? This whole time you're just hitting a pillow?"

"How was I supposed to know? I saw white. I couldn't stop and ask questions in the middle. We needed the element of surprise."

I held my hand up. "Wait a second." I looked around the room.

"What are you doing?" Tommy asked.

"Mr. Flopsy-Ears," I said.

Tommy cocked his head. "What?"

"The Cuddle Bunny. That's what Abby named him. It doesn't matter. He's not here."

Tommy looked around too. "Maybe she took him with her?"

I shook my head. "No, I made sure of it before she left. I watched her go. She wasn't holding Mr. Flopsy-Ears."

"Will you please stop saying Mr. Flopsy-Ears?"

"I'm sorry, but Abby talks to him all day long, so I have that stupid name stuck in my head."

"Whatever, it doesn't matter. First thing we have to do is find him."

"You think?"

He nodded. "You take the closet. I'll look through the rest of the room." Without waiting for me to answer, Tommy grabbed the side of Abby's bed. Because of all the bubble wrap he was wearing, he had to ease himself to the ground. He looked ridiculous, lowering himself at a forty-five-degree angle since he couldn't really bend his knees. "It's dark under here." He waved the bat back and forth under the bed. "Nothing."

I slid open the closet door and eyed all of Abby's things. Her clothes, which should have looked harmless hanging there, could now all be potential hiding spots for a killer bunny. I reached out slowly and with the tips of my fingers made snake-like strikes into Abby's clothes, ready just in case Mr. Flopsy-Ears jumped out. My heart pounded, but nothing happened.

Tommy appeared by my side.

"That's how you're looking?"

"What's wrong with it?"

He placed his hand on my chest and nudged me back. "Step aside, let me show you how it's done." He reared the bat back and swung hard, back and forth through the closet, sending Abby's clothes flying all over the place. Soccer uniforms zoomed by me like they were the closet's organs splattering everywhere. Some jackets hit my face. Tights fell to the floor by my feet. If the closet had been alive, Tommy had just murdered it. But still he kept swinging.

"Stop!" I said.

He didn't. Instead he just kept going and going until we heard a clanging sound.

Tommy and I stared at each other for only a second, because that's exactly how long it took for the bar across the top to come crashing down.

My hands flew to the top of my head and I grabbed two fistfuls of hair. "My mom is going to kill us."

"Relax, just tell her you don't know how it happened."

I stared at him. "I think the bubble wrap outfit and the bat in your hands might give it away."

"Well, duh! It's not going to be in my hands later."

"This isn't good. Help me pick everything up!"

We started scooping up clothes.

CREAK!

It came from behind us.

Tommy and I dropped the clothes.

A shadow crossed the wall of Abby's room.

We spun to see the door completely open and Mr. Flopsy-Ears lying in the doorway.

The next sound I heard is difficult to describe. The closest thing I could think of would be a cross between a screeching alley-cat and a wounded hyena. Unfortunately it came from neither of those. It was only after a few seconds that I realized it came from either Tommy or me, or maybe both. I actually wasn't sure, but either way, I wasn't proud. Especially when the next sound immediately after that was the popping when Tommy and I hugged for protection, popping many of the bubbles in our wrap.

"What's going on up there?" Dad shouted from downstairs.

I winced.

Tommy and I let go of each other.

"Shhh!" I said to Tommy. "Nothing, Dad! Just watching TV."

"TV? Well, it's too loud! Turn it down!"

"Okay, Dad!"

"And while you're at it, maybe do some chores."

"Okay, Dad!"

"Oh... and uh, just in case I fall asleep by accident, wake me when you see your mother pulling into the driveway."

"Okay, Dad!"

"Why didn't you tell him about the Cuddle Bunny?" Tommy asked.

"First of all, you're not even supposed to be here, and second, they already think I'm insane because of the Cuddle Bunny."

"Well, it wasn't there when we came in."

I stared at the stuffed animal on the floor. "Are you sure? Maybe we just ran by it because we rushed in?"

Tommy shook his head fast. "No way. It wasn't there. I would've seen it."

I knew he was right. The Cuddle Bunny wasn't there before, which was probably why my heart was playing a rock concert in my chest.

We inched forward, with Tommy holding the bat in front of him, until we reached the Cuddle Bunny.

Tommy poked Mr. Flopsy-Ears with the bat a couple of times, each time pulling it back fast, like someone testing a hot surface.

Mr. Flopsy-Ears didn't move.

We both exhaled.

Tommy lifted the Cuddle Bunny from the floor.

"Careful," I said.

He held it out in front of him while he looked it over. "It's okay, he looks harmless."

"I don't know," I said. "I'm telling you he's alive. I saw him wink. And stick out his tongue."

"Well, there's only one way to find out."

"What do you mean?"

"Get me a knife." Tommy said.

"A knife? What do you need a knife for?"

"Relax, I know what I'm doing. Do you have one or not?"

"Who keeps knives in their rooms? And I'm not going down to get one either. I don't want my dad waking up and asking too many questions."

"Well, I need something sharp." He paced back and forth. "I got it! Maybe we can break Abby's mirror and use a piece of the glass."

"*Are you crazy?* That's your solution? We're not breaking her mirror. Do you want me to be grounded for the rest of my life? And besides, isn't that supposed to be bad luck?"

He snorted. "Since when are you superstitious?"

"Me? What about you?"

"The stuff I do isn't superstition, it's based on fact."

"Yeah, okay."

He looked around the room again. "Well, if you don't want to break her mirror, what do you suggest we use?"

"First tell me what you're going to do."

He nodded toward the Cuddle Bunny. "I've done a lot of research on this."

"What's this?"

"Magically possessed toys."

"Where'd you research *that*?"

"Online. I did it right after you called me."

"How much research could you have done? It's not like this happens all the time."

Tommy blinked. "It happens way more than you think."

I sighed. Sometimes it was better to just let Tommy talk and get it over with. "Okay, so what did you find out?"

"First thing is, taking out their stuffing weakens them. If you take out enough, it could kill them. It's like their blood."

I eyed Mr. Flopsy-Ears and wondered what Abby's reaction would be if she came home and found a flattened piece of rabbit shell that used to be her Cuddle Bunny. "And what else?"

"Sounds."

"Sounds? Like what? What do you mean?"

"There are certain sounds they hate. And I mean can't stand. It seriously drives them crazy. If you do it loud enough, it can destroy them."

My eyes widened. "That sounds easy enough. Let's do that one."

He shook his head. "The problem is you never really know what sounds work with any given toy. We could try forever to find the right one. It's much better to just rip the stuffing out. It's quicker and easier."

I stared at the limp stuffed animal in his hand and weighed the consequences of getting in trouble for destroying Abby's FAB against the danger of letting it live and possibly one day killing us all in our sleep. I couldn't

90

take that chance. Mom and Dad would yell a little and Abby might cry, but at least I'd save everyone's life. "I think Abby has some scissors in here somewhere from her arts and crafts." I searched the room until I found a small pair on Abby's dresser, under several of her drawings. "Got 'em!" I offered them to Tommy.

Tommy took them from me and handed me the bat at the same time. "Here, you hold this." He examined the scissors and frowned. "These are rounded."

"Because they're children's scissors."

"I don't know if these are going to work, but I guess we have no choice." He clutched the pair of scissors like he was holding a knife. He held the rounded end above Mr. Flopsy-Ears. "Okay, on the count of three—"

I grabbed his wrist. "What are you going to do?"

"I'm going to tickle him, what do you think I'm going to do?"

I thought again of Mom and Dad's faces when they'd see what I had done to the Cuddle Bunny. "Okay, but maybe don't stab it."

"I don't even know if I can stab him with these. It'll probably just put a dent in him."

"But what if I'm wrong? You know how much trouble I'll get into? Couldn't you just cut along the seam? That way, in case we're wrong we could sew him up again."

Tommy let loud a loud sigh. "Fine, but you really can't go easy on these things." He turned the scissors over and opened them so one of the blades pressed against Mr. Flopsy-Ears' side. "Okay, here goes nothing."

Before Tommy could move, there was a white-streaked blur. Mr. Flopsy-Ears kicked the scissors away.

"Aaaaaaagh!" Tommy and I screamed.

Mr. Flopsy-Ears whirled and jumped out of Tommy's hand. In midair, he kicked out with both legs and struck Tommy and me in the head, sending us sprawling backwards. The bat flew out of my hands and crashed into the mirror. Shards of glass cascaded down onto Abby's dresser.

"Get him!" I screamed.

The large layers of plastic bubble wrap made moving difficult. Tommy and I bumped into each other. Several bubbles popped.

Mr. Flopsy-Ears scampered between my legs, grabbed one of my ankles, and flipped me up. I crashed into Tommy, who fell into the TV stand, which collapsed beneath his weight. Abby's television slid off and landed on the floor with a crash. The screen shattered.

"I thought I told you to turn that down!" Dad shouted from downstairs.

I couldn't answer, even if I'd wanted to.

The Cuddle Bunny was on me, paws clutching my throat, strangling me. I saw my panicked reflection in his black button eyes.

"Urrgh!" A gurgling sound escaped my lips.

"Hold on, I got you!" Tommy said.

The Cuddle Bunny, using his feet to feet to push off of me, maintained his hold on my throat and kicked backwards into Tommy's stomach.

"Oof!" Tommy grunted as he went flying into Abby's dresser. Several pops. The plastic made him bounce off, where he staggered a moment until he fell on top of me.

The Cuddle Bunny jumped onto both of us and smacked us repeatedly with his ears, using them like the flippers in a pinball machine.

"What's going on up there?" Dad asked. "Is someone else there?" His footsteps stomped up the staircase.

Mr. Flopsy-Ears spun fast toward the sound, his long ears whipping behind him. He hopped off of us and bounded toward the window. He slid it open and leaped out to the tree.

"After him!" I shouted and hobbled to my feet.

Dad appeared in the doorway. He looked back and forth between Tommy and me and then seemed to finally take in the destruction in the room. His jaw dropped. *"What did you two do in here?"* He eyed our outfits. "And what in the world are you wearing?"

I rushed by him. "No time now, Dad. It's an emergency. I'll explain later."

Tommy and I raced to the stairs. Unfortunately, our outfits were not the type that allowed for racing. I'm not sure who collided with who, but our feet caught and we went tumbling down the staircase. Like the sound of a rapid-fire machine-gun, pops of plastic bubbles went off like exploding bullets as we rolled from step to step until we landed with a thud at the bottom.

I groaned for a moment, but mostly felt okay. As much as I hated to admit it, Tommy had been right. The outfits had protected us. Not from a crazed killer bunny, but from each other. I grabbed the railing and pulled myself to my feet and waddled to the front door, with Tommy at my heels.

I yanked it open and jumped onto the porch, just in time to see Mr. Flopsy-Ears scamper across the street into Herb's yard. Without a word, the front door opened and the Cuddle Bunny disappeared inside, the door closing behind him.

"No!"

Tommy panted beside me. "We have to stop him."

Before we could even take a step, a hand gripped each of us, like talons on our shoulders.

I turned to see Dad standing behind us.

"You two aren't going anywhere."

CHAPTER NINE

THE WARLOCK WILL SEE YOU NOW

I had to admit that if I would've known what my punishment was going to be, I probably would've let the Bunny kill me. I shouldn't have even been surprised when he walked in. Because really, who else *would* it be?

"Thanks again for coming over, Herb," Mom said.

I sat on the couch, while he took the recliner. It was Mom's idea. She said I would be comfortable that way. If by "comfortable" she meant the same sensation you got while a dentist drilled your teeth, then she was right.

I had no idea what this was all about, but I wanted it to be over with as soon as possible.

Herb looked over to me. "I want you to know that as a matter of practice, anything you say will be kept strictly confidential."

"Confidential?" I turned to Mom. "*He's a psychiatrist?*"

"Oh, heavens no." Herb chuckled. "I'm a therapist. I don't prescribe anything. This isn't even an official therapy session. I'm just here to talk. Or actually, let you talk and I'll listen."

"I don't need a therapist!"

"Sweetie, nobody said you did," Mom said. "It's only to talk."

Herb smiled. "Just a friendly little chat."

The light reflected off Herb's glasses, hiding his eyes.

I stared at him, trying to figure what he was up to, but it was no use. The only thing I could think of was that maybe I could trick him. Get him to slip and reveal himself to be a warlock in front of Mom. Still, I'd have to be on guard. Warlocks were sneaky. "Okay, Mom. I'll do it."

"Fantastic!" Herb clapped. "Now, you just relax and don't worry about a thing. It's nothing more than you and me having a nice little rap. Just two buddies talking. Two amigos, if you will."

"Okaaaay." I glanced at Mom to try to get across just how stupid this was, but she turned and went to the kitchen.

Herb looked at me and smirked. "How are you, Devin?"

For some reason, I scooted back in my seat. "I-I don't know what you're doing, Herb, but I'm going to find out."

"What is it that you think I'm doing?"

I had to think a second. I realized I wasn't exactly sure what it was that I thought he was doing. I knew he had somehow brought the Cuddle Bunny to life, but I still didn't know why. What did he have to gain by it? It couldn't just be to spy on me. I never do anything worth checking out. But why, then?

Mom suddenly appeared by Herb's side and offered him a cup. "Tea?"

Herb accepted. "Thank you so much! I love tea." He blew across the top, sending a trail of steam into the air before taking a loud, slurping sip. "Oh, this really hits the spot. There's nothing like a good hot cup of tea. Why, in many cultures the act of drinking tea together is considered more a symbolic ritual of friendship, than just simply people partaking in the sharing of a brewed beverage."

It was official. Every time he spoke, I had absolutely no idea what he was talking about.

Herb took another sip and then set the teacup down on the coffee table, reached inside his jacket, and pulled out a small notebook and pen. "Okay, what can old Herb help you with?"

Mom pulled up a chair on the other side of him and sat. "It's just . . ." She glanced at me. "Well, it's the Cuddle Bunny, Herb."

Finally, an opportunity to get this all out and let her see for herself what Herb was up to.

Herb cocked his head. "The *Cuddle Bunny*?" He tapped his chest. "The Cuddle Bunny I bought? I don't understand, is there something wrong with it?"

Mom shook her head. "No, it's not that, it's just . . ."

"Just what?" His eyebrows arched above the frames of his glasses. "Oooooh, I think I get it now." He jotted something into the notebook and placed his hands over his heart. "Devin, I apologize from the bottom of my heart. Honestly, it never occurred to me that you might want a Cuddle Bunny too, because if I would've known, I surely—"

"What?" I asked. "No! I don't want a Cuddle Bunny!"

He leaned back again. "Oh, so what seems to be the trouble?"

Mom eyed me once more. She looked like she was trying to find the right thing to say. Finally, she cupped her hands around her mouth and whispered. "He thinks the Cuddle Bunny is alive."

"Mom, I'm sitting right here. I can hear you!"

She threw her arms out to the side. "Well, I'm sorry. I just don't know how else to say it."

Herb jotted down more notes. "I see. This is very interesting."

"What is?" I asked. "What's interesting? What are you writing?"

He ignored me. "So, if I'm to understand this correctly, you have attributed life-qualities to a stuffed animal?" He tapped his pen against his forehead. "Fascinating."

"What is it?" Mom asked. "Please, tell me."

He waved her off. "Not to worry, I've seen this before."

Mom perked up. "You have?"

Herb nodded. "It's called Anthropomorphizing Syndrome."

98

Mom gasped. "Oh, my. Is it serious?"

"Well, it means that Devin is giving living characteristics to inanimate objects, such as the Cuddle Bunny. It could just be a phase, but . . ." He looked over at me and held his gaze for a moment before speaking. "It's also possible that this could be part of a more serious underlying issue."

"That's ridiculous," I shouted. "I didn't give living characteristics to it! You did!" I looked at Mom. "He brought the Cuddle Bunny to life."

Okay, thinking back to what I just said, I realized that there was absolutely no way to say that without sounding insane. Still, I had to find some way to make Mom believe me and unfortunately, the only way I could think of to do that was to keep going along and hope to somehow trap Herb in his lies.

Mom waited a second more before turning back to Herb. "So . . . I think you see what I was talking about.

Herb nodded. "Hmmmm, yes . . ." More jotting. "But don't worry yet." He tapped the side of his head. "This might just be his mind's way of saying, 'Hey, Devin, something's not right here in my noggin, so I'm just going to say some kooky things and hopefully, somebody will notice and get me fixed.'"

Mom brought her hand up to her mouth, a look of concern on her face. "I knew something was wrong. Is there anything you can do to help him?"

Herb pyramided his fingers in front of his face, closed his eyes, and finally nodded. "It won't be easy, but I do believe I can."

Mom exhaled. "Oh, I knew you could, Herb. That's why I called you. What do you need us to do?"

"Well, first thing I need is to see this 'dangerous'"—he made finger quotes in the air—"Cuddle Bunny."

"I can't," I said. "Because he's at your house."

Herb's eyebrows furrowed. "My house? Why would it be at my house?"

"Because we saw Mr. Flopsy-Ears run across the street and into your home." Yeah, I heard how stupid that sounded too, but I was already too far in to stop now.

"Mr. Flopsy-Ears?" Herb asked.

"Oh, that's what Abby named her Cuddle Bunny," Mom said.

Herb clapped his hands together and laughed. "What a delightful name. Why, I remember when I was a young buck, I had a stuffed bear named Wilbur."

"That's adorable," Mom said.

"It is?" I asked.

Mom glared at me, but Herb didn't seem to notice.

Instead, he just kept going. "I named him after a character from one of my favorite teevee shows."

Mom's face lit up. "Oh, the one with the talking horse?"

Herb gasped. "Talking horse? That does sound funny, but no. I'm talking about *Wilbur Pickles*. Well, Pickles wasn't really his last name, it was Claremont, but everybody called him Wilbur Pickles, because—"

Mom cut in. "—he liked pickles?"

100

Herb's face lit up. "Like? No sirree." He laughed again. "He loooooved pickles! I mean, he wolfed them down like they were going out of style. That show just tickled my funny-bone like nobody's business."

I buried my face in my hands. "Can we please get back to Mr. Flopsy-Ears?" I looked up at Mom. "I'm telling you, the Cuddle Bunny ran to his house. I know how it sounds, but I saw it!"

Herb stared at me a moment and then picked up the notebook and scribbled something inside. "How long have you been feeling that your toys were alive?"

"I don't think my toys are alive."

Herb slid his finger along the bridge of his nose to push his glasses up. "But you think the Cuddle Bunny is?"

I glanced back and forth between Mom and Herb. I needed to turn this around. Make Herb answer questions. "So, then where is he? Where is Mr. Flopsy-Ears?"

Herb shrugged. "Devin, I'm not sure how you would expect me to know something like that. I haven't seen the Cuddle Bunny since I gave him to Abby as a gift. If you'd like, you are more than welcome to come to my house to look for it. But in the meantime, if it brings you some peace, it'd be my pleasure to get another one. For you too, if you'd like."

Mom waved her hands in front of her. "Herb, no. If the kids can't take care of their things, then they shouldn't be rewarded for losing them."

"Oh, I quite agree. Spare the rod and spoil the child, I always say." He looked out the corner of his eye at me. "A firm hand is sometimes needed to guide them through life's pitfalls." He picked up the notebook again. "We have to do whatever we can to help poor Devin. It takes a village, you know."

Mom clasped her hands together. "I knew you could help. So, what should we do first?"

Herb cleared his throat and leaned forward again. "I think we should have another 'chat.'" Again with the finger quotes. "You know," Herb continued. "Until this passes."

"What?" I shook my head. "I am *not* seeing Herb for any sessions."

"Whoa!" Herb held his hands up. "Nobody said anything about any sessions. These are just chats. An informal get-together." He shrugged. "I wouldn't have a formal session with a friend. This is just a conversation between neighbors. Nothing to be alarmed about."

"I know this isn't just a conversation, Herb. You're not fooling me."

"Excuse me?" Herb said.

I pointed at him. "You can save the act. I know Mr. Flopsy-Ears attacked us. He jumped me and Tommy and popped our bubbles."

"Bubbles?" Herb asked.

"Um . . ." Mom hesitated. "I don't know why, but they were wearing bubble wrap for some reason."

More scribbling. "I see. Is this something you do often?"

"*Where is heeeeeeee?*" A high-decibel shriek.

Abby.

The drumbeat of footsteps rushing down the staircase, seconds before Abby exploded into the room. Out in front of her, arms extended, like she was holding a fresh kill, was one gray, big-mouthed Hugging Hippo.

"*Where is my Cuddle Bunny?*" Abby demanded. She hurled the Hugging Hippo across the room, where it smashed into a wall with a splat and slid to the ground.

The stupid Hugging Hippo song went off.

I'm a Hugging Hippo
I'm your Hugging friend
We'll always be together
I'll follow you to the end

Abby wailed. It was forced, but Mom acted like it was the end of the world and bolted out of her seat and ran to her. "Honey, what's wrong?"

"You can't be buying this," I said.

Mom glared at me.

Yep, she bought it.

Abby pointed to the lifeless, mangled stuffed animal on the ground. "That's a Hugging Hippo. They're stupid. They're baby toys." Her nostrils flared. She gritted her teeth. "Devin destroyed my room and stole my Cuddle Bunny. I want my Cuddle Bunny!"

Mom stared at the FAB. "Wait a minute. Where'd you get a Hugging Hippo from?"

Out of the corner of my eye I saw a figure enter the room. We all turned to see Dad standing there.

His eyes flicked back and forth between all of us. "Um, I, uh . . . think I left something in the car." He tried to backpedal out of the room.

"Don't move!" Mom said.

Dad's Adam's apple rolled down his throat. "Hey, babe. Wow, you look beautiful today. What's going on, did I miss anything?"

Mom put her hands on her hips and thrust her chin forward. "Did you buy her a Hugging Hippo?"

Dad turned to look behind him, but there was nobody there. He pointed to his chest. "Are you talking to me?"

Mom's eyes narrowed.

He held up his hands. "Okay, okay." He nodded. "Yes, I bought it. I didn't want her upset, so I went to buy another FAB, but they were still out of the Cuddle Bunnies, so I got her a Hugging Hippo. What's the big deal? Aren't they all the same?"

Abby stomped her foot. "They are NOT the same! Nobody plays with Hugging Hippos anymore! They're stupid. They look stupid. Their song is stupid. They're stupid."

"Oh, I don't know," Dad said. "I kind of like the song." He began to sing. "I will hug you, I will squeeze you, I will never let you go."

I didn't think it was possible, but Dad actually made the song worse.

Abby covered her ears. "STOP!" She stomped her foot again. "I hate that song. I hate the Hugging Hippos. Cuddle Bunnies don't even like the Hugging Hippos and they like everyone."

"Abby, that's silly," Dad said. "I'm sure Cuddle Bunnies and Hugging Hippos are the best of friends."

"No they aren't! On last week's show, all the Cuddle Bunnies in FABville were bullied by the mean Hugging Hippos, so they got together to kick them out. They're at war now."

"War?" Dad asked. "This is a children's show? I don't think those are the right kind of values they should be teaching—"

"I WANT MY CUDDLE BUNNY!" Abby screamed.

"But they don't have any right now," Dad said.

Abby's head swiveled slowly toward me. It seemed to extend beyond what a normal human girl should be capable of. Another inch or two, and she'd be spitting pea soup and we'd have to call an exorcist to deal with her.

Her eyes locked onto me.

I had to admit that I was far more frightened of an eight-year-old girl than I should've been. By the looks on Mom and Dad's faces, I wasn't the only one.

Abby's hands balled into little fists. "You did this," she hissed. "You did something to Mr. Flopsy-Ears."

I don't know why, but I shrank back into the couch. I wished it went back further. "I didn't do anything. The Cuddle Bunny ran away on his own. You don't believe me, but he was dangerous."

Abby pointed at me. "Devin, if I don't get my Cuddle Bunny back, you're going to pay."

Herb stood up from the recliner. "Adorable child." He patted her head. "Anyhoo, I think it best that I leave now, so you can deal with this mounting crisis."

"But what about Devin?" Mom asked.

"Oh, I'm not forgetting." Herb smiled. "I just know the loss of a loved one—in this case, Mr. Flopsy-Ears—can have a traumatic effect on a young child. I think your family needs to deal with it and see how it makes all of you feel." He looked down at Abby. "For the sake of the little one."

"Um," Dad interrupted. "We are aware that it's just a toy, right?"

"It's not a toy!" I said. "It's an evil, maniac stuffed animal, which Herb created to kill us all."

Mom turned to Herb. "Seriously, what are we going to do about Devin?"

Herb flipped the pages of his notebook. "Well, I am swamped, but I'll make an exception for you since we're all such good friends now." He shook Mom's hand. "How about you bring Devin over tomorrow to my house? Let's say noon? It's perhaps best to get him away from this setting, which is clearly causing him some distress."

Mom nodded. "That'd be great, Herb. Thanks so much."

"What?" I jumped up from the couch. "I'm not going." I turned to Dad. "Dad, you have to do something."

"Devin's right," Dad said. "How much will this cost?"

"Oh, heavens," Herb said. "For neighbors it's free. I just want to help poor Devin get better."

"Free?" Dad asked. "Okay, then he'll be there."

"What?" I threw my hands up. "This is ridiculous!"

Herb leaned down to Abby and tapped her on her nose. "And don't you worry. I'm sure your Cuddle Bunny will turn up soon."

"He'd better." She glared at me before storming out of the room.

"Well, I'm afraid I have to be off too," Herb said. "I just hope I'm able to help."

"You already have, Herb." Mom said. "Let me walk you to the door."

"Thank you kindly," Herb said and then turned to point at me. "And you, I'll see tomorrow." Herb winked and walked out of the room.

CHAPTER TEN

INTO THE WARLOCK'S LAIR

I paced the floor of my room so much that I had worn a path on the carpet. Every so often I'd stop and peek out the window at Herb's house, but it was too dark to really see anything. I'd spent hours trying to convince Mom and Dad that they shouldn't take me there and even longer trying to convince Abby that I didn't do anything to Mr. Flopsy-Ears.

I'm not sure any of them believed me. With Mom and Dad, every time it came down to the reason I didn't think I needed therapy, I didn't exactly help myself by mentioning how Herb was responsible for bringing the Cuddle Bunny to life to kill us. Actually, I think it made them feel like I needed it even more.

Without proof, Mom and Dad weren't going to do anything. I had to get some, but I had no idea how.

A knock on the door. I jumped.

I turned to see Tommy standing in my doorway, carrying a backpack.

"What are you doing here?" I asked.

"I'm sleeping over. Didn't your mom tell you?"

I shook my head. "No. She's too busy sending me to Herb for therapy."

"What?" Tommy asked. "What are you talking about?"

I shrugged. "Well, they say it's not therapy, but I know better. They're calling it a 'chat.'" I made air quotes. "Unbelievable, I'm doing it too now."

Tommy cocked his head. "What?"

I waved him off. "Nothing. Anyway, they're so upset about everything that's happened, they think I have issues."

"So, why Herb?"

"Because he's a therapist. Seriously, what kind of a warlock is a therapist?" I stared at him for a moment. "Wait a second, how are you even allowed out? Do you ever get in trouble for anything?"

Tommy shrugged. "Nah, not really. I think I drive my parents so crazy, they prefer when I'm out. I think that's why they send me over here a lot."

I sighed. "I hadn't noticed."

"Anyway, get back to the stuff about Herb. What's the deal with that?"

I filled him in on everything that had happened. Unlike Mom and Dad, he didn't look like he had any trouble believing me at all. After I finished, he just stood there in silence, looking down and rubbing his chin.

"Well?" I said. "Aren't you going to say anything?"

Tommy motioned for quiet. "Please, I must have total silence to concentrate." He paced the room with his hands clasped behind his back. He looked like a detective in those old movies.

"Seriously?"

"Shhhh!" He paced some more and then suddenly stopped and looked at me. A wide grin spread across his face. He reminded me of the Cheshire Cat from *Alice in Wonderland*. "I got it."

"What?"

"Herb just gave us the way to beat him and doesn't even know it."

"What do you mean?"

"His house!" Tommy said. "He asked you to go into his house."

"Yeah, for therapy."

Tommy nodded. "Yeah, for you, but not for me."

"What are you talking about?"

"You go in for therapy and keep him busy, while I search the place."

"That's your plan? How are you going to get inside? You can't break in, you know. It's against the law."

"Stop worrying. Nobody is going to catch me. Remember how back in third grade they always called me 'shadow' because I was so good at hiding?"

"What are you talking about?" I rolled my eyes. "They called you 'shadow' because you always followed me around."

"Let's just agree to disagree about that. Now, do you want to hear my plan or not?"

"Your plan is stupid. First of all, you can't break in to someone's house. And second, I don't want to go for therapy. Especially not there. I mean, did you ever wonder why he's asking me to go to begin with? He's probably going to kill me."

"Nah, not with your mom there." He thought a second. "Well, unless he kills her too. But still, your dad knows you guys will be there. That'd be an awful lot of trouble to go through just to kill you guys now. I mean, think about it, it's not easy to kill someone. And then he'd have to come to your house after and kill your dad and probably Abby too." He shook his head. "Nope, it'd just be easier for him to wait till later, when the Cuddle Bunny could just sneak in and wipe all of you out in one night. It just makes sense. So, I think you're probably safe. I'm like 75 percent sure of it."

"Oh, I feel a lot better now, thanks."

He swatted my chest. "Stop worrying. I know everything there is to know about warlocks."

"No, you don't."

"You don't know all the things I know. I've studied this for a long time."

"Why would you study that?"

He snorted. "Are you serious? In Gravesend, you *have* to know about this stuff! A lot of weird stuff happens here."

"Like what?"

"Just trust me. This town's always been weird, and besides, I have the perfect thing for warlocks." He reached into his backpack and pulled out a vial. "I got this."

I groaned. "Please tell me that it's not more of your 'holy water.'"

"This is different. This stuff's the real deal. My neighbor, Mr. Merrin, used to be a priest and blessed it for me."

I eyed the vial. "I don't know."

He looked into my eyes a moment, then glanced at the vial and nodded. "Trust me. I'm, like, almost sure it'll work."

"It's really bothering me about what you mean by 'used to' be a priest."

He flipped his hand to wave me off. "Don't worry about that. The point is, I have this as a 'just in case.' If anything happens . . . *Boom!* I whip out the vial, spray Herb, he disintegrates, and everyone is happy. The end."

My head was pounding from listening to him. "Yeah, I don't see anything that could possibly go wrong with that."

"Will you stop being so negative? Now, here's the plan . . ." He motioned me to come closer.

I looked back over my shoulder and around the room. "There's nobody else here."

Tommy pointed up and twirled his hand in a circle above his head. "The walls have ears."

I pinched the bridge of my nose and closed my eyes. With Tommy, it was always only a matter of time before he gave me a migraine. "Will you just say it?"

"Okay, tomorrow, when you go for your therapy, make sure the door stays unlocked. Then, I wait for like ten or fifteen minutes and sneak into his house and search the place. I'll give you some signal or something when I'm done."

"A signal?"

"Yeah, like maybe a bird-call or something. Like caw-caw. Caw-caw."

"Why would a crow be in his house?"

"It's a raven."

"That's not a raven, it's a crow sound."

"Why would I make a crow sound?"

"Why would you make any sound?" I asked.

"Shhhh!" He motioned for me to keep quiet. "We need to have a signal."

I was sure the veins in my forehead were throbbing. "What are you looking for anyway?"

He shrugged. "I don't know. I guess I'll figure it out when I see it."

I walked to my bed and plopped down. "Forget it. This is stupid. You don't even know what you're looking for."

"We'll be fine. I promise." He held a fist out to me and shook it. "Anyway, let's rock-paper-scissors it to see who gets the bed."

I threw a pillow at him and pointed to the ground. "It's my bed, I get it. You can have the floor." I turned away from him. "And turn the light off while you're up."

"It's only like nine o'clock!"

"I'm tired, and this day has given me a huge headache."

"*Hmmmph.* You're the worst host ever."

I heard rustling behind me, but didn't turn to see what he was doing. I don't know how long I was lying there before the lights finally went out and didn't care. I wasn't sleeping anyway. All I could do was stare into the darkness and think about just how disastrous tomorrow was going to be.

"Stop fidgeting!" Mom hissed. She patted down my hair. "You can't look like a bum."

We stood on the sidewalk in front of Herb's house. It was cold, and I was bundled up in two sweaters and a coat. A heavy wind blew, and there was a fresh coating of snow on the ground. I hadn't realized just how thick the hedges that surrounded Herb's place were. It made it seem like a walled-in fortress.

A shadow crossed the yard. I looked up to see dark clouds rolling in. I could've sworn the sky was clear a few moments ago. More gathered. It looked like they were trying to swallow the sun. This did not give me a very good feeling.

I turned my attention back to his house. Even though I lived across the street, this was the first time I was taking a good look at it. From here, it seemed like any other house in the neighborhood, but it sure didn't feel like it. With the surrounding hedges and the way the shadows passed over, it felt a whole lot creepier than anyplace else. It's amazing how many things are right around you that you never pay attention to, until you're about to get disintegrated to ashes by an evil, scheming warlock.

Mom started up the path to Herb's house and dragged me behind her. I stepped into a shadow from one of the hedges. It felt like ice water shot through me and I shivered. If Mom felt it too, she didn't let on, since she continued pulling me along until we reached the front door.

I tried to wrench my arm away from her, but she held tight. "I don't want to go!"

"You promised me!" she said. "Now stop squirming and stand still." She rang the bell.

Music played.

Mom and I looked at each other.

"Wait a second," I said. "I know that song."

Mom nodded. "Yes, that's—"

The door opened.

"*The Addams Family.*" Herb chuckled. "That's just my macabre sense of humor. Kids will love it come Halloween time. Anyhoo, where are your manners, Herbert T. Dorfman?" He jabbed his finger at me. "The 'T' stands for Time to get you better! Come on in!" He extended his arm into the house.

"Thank you, Herb," Mom said and walked in, keeping my wrist in a vise-like grip.

"You have to forgive my appearance," Herb said. "I was just pumping iron in my workout room. Your body is your temple, as they say. But don't let this physique intimidate you. Sure, I may look like Charles Atlas on the outside, but on the inside, I'm still plain old Herb."

I noticed for the first time that he was wearing gym shorts and a tank top that draped over him. It was at least three sizes too big. It read FUTURE MR. OLYMPIA across the front. He wore a blue sweatband above his eyes, which was dark in spots from the sweat trickling down his forehead. His glasses were fogged up, making it difficult to see his eyes.

"That's good to know," I said under my breath.

"Should we come back later?" Mom asked.

"Oh, heavens no!" Herb laughed. "Let's do this. Mind over muscles, I always say. Please come in."

I crossed into Herb's hallway and glanced up at him.

The corner of his mouth twitched up.

I took a peek behind me to see if I could spot Tommy anywhere, but he was nowhere to be found.

Herb placed his hand on the door and slowly pushed it closed.

I watched as the triangle of light that made its way into the house from outside, shrank until only a sliver was left, before it was finally extinguished into darkness. I realized, I couldn't tell if he locked it or not.

"I know it's a little dark in here," Herb said. "But there'll be plenty of light ahead."

I felt Herb's hand on my back nudging me along through the shadows. Mom was a couple of steps ahead and oblivious to it all. I had no idea what to expect and was, for some reason, relying on Tommy and a plan of his to come through for me.

The thought hit and sank in.

I was relying on a plan of Tommy's to come through.

CHAPTER ELEVEN

THE WARLOCK, THE BUNNY, AND THE SOCK

I'm not sure what I expected Herb's office to be like, but I never expected to go down a flight of stairs to get there. He said he had a basement office, but walking down made it feel like I was being taken to a dungeon. It was the most non-threatening dungeon ever, though. If anything, considering how weird he was, his office was completely normal.

Well, maybe normal wasn't exactly the right word. It reminded me of the time I visited my grandmother's house in Boca Raton, Florida. Herb had some pink lacy things draped over the sofas and little porcelain statuettes of some fat babies with wings in several spots around the room.

The room was large and mostly dark, lit only by a lamp on an end table next to a big pink armchair with oversized cushions. Pictures hung on the walls. I had thought the winged fat babies were creepy until I saw the paintings.

Most were hidden in shadows, but from the ones I could see, they were all portraits of Herb, dressed in clothes from different times. Like costumes or something. Weirdo.

There were a couple of little windows up near the top of the walls, but they were covered fully by drapes. Mom sat across from me, and I lay on a couch next to the pink chair, which Herb was sitting on. The lamp had a little shade with flowers on it, which was tilted at an angle to shine light at Herb. The scene was eerily similar to the one at my house yesterday, except now I wasn't safe in my living room. I was in the lion's den, or spider's web, or whatever place it was where warlocks trapped you.

I looked over at Herb. He was sitting with one leg crossed over the other and was still in a tank top and shorts. For some reason, all I could think of was his sweat making him stick to the leather chair. The thought made my stomach turn. He placed his notebook on his knee. He was jotting something down and we hadn't even started yet.

"What are you writing now?" I asked.

"Oh, it's nothing," Herb said. "Just some notes to remind me later of what was said. Stuff I wouldn't want to bore you with." He smiled at Mom. "And don't you worry about a thing. He's going to be right as rain in no time. Soon we won't even remember that he had any problems."

"I don't have any problems," I said. "I'm not crazy."

"Devin," Mom said. "Nobody said anything about being crazy."

Herb wagged his finger. "No sirree, Bob. The C word is a big no-no around here. Right now, I think you're just going through some stress. Making you see things a little . . ." He waved his fingers in the air. "Kooky."

"What should I do, Herb?" Mom asked.

"Don't worry," he said. "Right now, we're just going to hear what's on Devin's mind, that's all. This isn't even therapy. It's just some more in-depth chatting. A little tête-à-tête, except with three people."

"A what?" I asked.

She nodded. "I understand."

I turned to her. "You do?"

"Just relax, Devin," she said. "I'm going to stay here the whole time."

Herb nodded. "I agree. We want Devin to be as comfortable as possible, and the way to do that is for you to hear *everything* that's said." He looked over to me. "After all, we want your mother to know what's going on, don't we?"

"You're very kind, Herb," Mom said. "And don't worry, I'll just sit back, listen, and you won't even know I'm here. I'll be a fly on the wall." She pretended to zip her lips and leaned back in her chair.

"Very well." Herb turned to me. "Devinnnnn . . ." He stretched out my name. "You are in a safe and protective environment. Everyone is your friend. We are here for you. There are no 'gotchas' here." He made air quotes.

"Everything that's said is for your benefit. Now, tell me about your hatred of Cuddle Bunnies."

"I don't hate Cuddle Bunnies!" I said. "But this isn't a normal Cuddle Bunny!"

"I see." More jotting. "So, it's Mr. Flopsy-Ears you hate."

"Yeah, because Mr. Flopsy-Ears is a psycho little rabbit."

Herb rubbed his chin. "Devin, I think I'm beginning to understand what this is about."

Mom leaned forward again. "What is it, Herb?"

"Devin, your mother loves you very much." He looked at her and nodded.

"What?" Mom asked. "What do I do?"

Herb motioned toward me. "Reaffirm your love for Devin."

"Oh!" Mom said. "Sorry, Devin. Yes, Mommy loves you very much."

"Oh, brother," I said.

"Good." Herb nodded. "Devin, I think you're tying Mr. Flopsy-Ears to your resentment of Abby for taking part of your mother's love. The affection that Abby shows Mr. Flopsy-Ears reminds you of the undivided attention that you used to get from your mother."

I sat up on the couch. "Mom, really? Are you listening to any of this? I'm not saying another word. This is ridiculous."

"This is quite natural," Herb whispered. "I've seen it before. It's a stage of resistance. Let's help him fight through it, so we can acknowledge what's going on and resolve it."

Mom glanced at Herb before reaching out to me like she was pleading. "Devin, I don't know if that's what you're feeling or not, but I think Herb is only trying to help. Maybe you should talk to him?"

I shook my head. "Mom, in case you didn't realize, I can hear him talking to you. I'm sitting right here. He's fooling you. You can't trust him."

"Devin," Mom pleaded. "He's only trying to help."

Herb held up his hand. "It's okay, really. I know all about these kids and their 'Don't trust anyone over the age of thirty' feelings. Sometimes children just aren't comfortable talking to grown-ups. We're not 'groovy.'" He made finger quotes in the air. "Or 'far out,' if you will. Well, don't you fear, because I have just the solution for that." He leaned over the side of his chair, away from me, and started digging around. "In my experiences, children need someone they can relate to." He twisted his arm back and forth several times. "And here we go." He pulled his arm up, only it was now encased in a white sock, with two button eyes and bushy white eyebrows and mustache. Where the fingers were, there was a toy cigar glued to the mouth. "Perhaps, you'd feel more comfortable talking to my colleague, Dr. Sockmund Freud?"

My jaw dropped. I stared at the sock, and then looked back at Mom. "Seriously?"

"Devin, Herb's a professional. I'm sure he knows what he's doing. It's worth a try, no?" Her eyes seemed sincere.

I couldn't believe she was buying this. "I'm not talking to a sock."

"Doctor." Herb nodded toward it. "It's Doctor Sockmund."

I threw my hands up. "It's a sock!" Before I could continue, something behind Mom hopped across the room near another sofa. The Cuddle Bunny. I jumped up and pointed. "Mr. Flopsy-Ears!"

Mom and Herb whirled to where I was pointing, but the Cuddle Bunny had jumped behind the sofa.

My heart thumped. I ran to the spot.

Nothing.

"Devin, what are you doing?" Mom asked.

I circled the sofa twice and jabbed my finger into the air. "He was here! Mr. Flopsy-Ears was here. I told you he was."

Mom glanced at Herb.

He shrugged. Wrote some more in his notebook.

She turned back to me. "Devin, sweetie . . . we don't see a Cuddle Bunny here. Maybe you just thought you saw him?"

"No! He was here. He was hopping across the floor." Okay, that time I also heard how ludicrous it sounded.

Herb shrugged. "Devin, I don't know what happened to Mr. Flopsy-Ears, but why would I take a stuffed animal that I gave to your sister as a gift? It doesn't make sense."

I ignored him and dropped to the ground to look under the sofa. Still nothing. "It's got to be here somewhere."

Herb cleared his throat. "Devin, let's sit down and talk. I think you've been under a lot of stress lately."

"I'm telling you, he was right here."

Herb motioned for me to go back to the couch. "Come, have a seat."

I took baby steps, training my eyes back on the sofa the whole time. Beads of sweat trickled down my forehead. I sat back down. I had definitely seen Mr. Flopsy-Ears, but how could he have disappeared so fast?

"So, Devin," Herb began. "Why don't you tell us what's bothering you? Something at school? Perhaps at home?"

"Is there anything, Devin?" Mom interrupted. "Have I done something? You could tell us."

"Yes, Devin," Herb said. "Tell me. Tell us." He nodded toward his hand. "Tell Dr. Sockmund."

I looked back and forth between Mom and Herb and Dr. Sockmund.

She forced a smile. The kind that she gave when I was sick and went to the doctor and promised I wouldn't need a shot. I always knew I was going to get one anyway.

Then there was Herb. His smile wasn't fake at all.

No, his smile was very real. He was enjoying this. He was lying and I knew it, but what was he up to?

Out of the corner of my eye, a flash of white. I turned toward it. By the sofa. First came the ears, followed by the eyes. He peered out from behind the sofa. His ears wiggled and he waved.

I looked at Herb and his smile widened.

Dr. Sockmund's head cocked to the side.

Suddenly, the Bunny was behind Mom. She was staring at me and didn't see it.

I looked past her and straight at it.

Mr. Flopsy-Ears put his little paws up and started swaying back and forth. He wiggled his tail and started dancing.

I glanced at Herb.

His teeth beamed like a lighthouse in the harbor. His eyebrows arched. "Is anything wrong, Devin?" He was loving this. He wanted me to look bad in front of Mom. This whole thing was a setup.

I turned back to the Cuddle Bunny.

Mom leaned forward. "Devin, why aren't you answering Herb?" She followed my gaze.

Mr. Flopsy-Ears dove behind the sofa again.

Mom turned to look behind her. "What do you keep looking at?"

I wanted to tell her again. To scream it. But I knew it'd be no use. I knew if I ran over there, he'd just disappear again. I had to wait, time this right, and pounce. Catch that psycho little rabbit. I winced. I had become Elmer Fudd.

Mom turned back to me. "Devin? What's going on?"

Mr. Flopsy-Ears popped out again. He waved both paws this time, across each other, like he was trying to get my attention. He had it. He hopped toward me.

"Devin." Herb moved Dr. Sockmund's mouth. "I'm here to help you."

"I'm not talking to a stupid—"

I stopped short. Mr. Flopsy-Ears hopped closer. He put his paws up by his ears and stuck out his tongue.

"Devin, what are you doing?" She turned again, but the Cuddle Bunny leaped behind her chair in time. "What's over there that's so fascinating?"

Herb shielded his mouth with his hand and whispered to Mom, loud enough for me to hear, "He's escaping from reality again."

"I can hear you!" I said.

"Devin, as a friend and a professional, it is my opinion that you need to say what you're feeling."

Mom nodded. "Yes, Devin. For me."

I rolled my eyes. I didn't know what I could do to get out of this. I was talking to a sneaky warlock with a sock on his hand, while a deranged killer bunny was on the loose and my mom couldn't see any of it. Could this get any weirder?

I decided to play this out in the hopes of catching Mr. Flopsy-Ears. "*Fine*. What do you want to know, Herb?"

Herb pointed to his hand. "Dr. Sockmund. You need to speak to Dr. Sockmund."

I sighed. Well, it just got weirder. "What do you want to know, Dr. Sockmund?"

Mom clasped her hands and smiled. "Thank you, Devin."

From right behind Mom, two ears rose, like the periscope of a submarine emerging from the water. Mr. Flopsy-Ears leaned out so I could see his face over Mom's shoulder. He wasn't smiling this time. His fluffy white eyebrows furrowed. His button eyes narrowed into slits. His paws reached out on either side of Mom's neck. Near her throat.

"Get away from her!" I leaped from the couch straight at Mom's chair.

"Devin!" Mom screamed, right before I knocked the seat over trying to get at the Cuddle Bunny.

"Oh, my!" I heard Herb yell.

Mom went sprawling to the ground, but I managed to grab Mr. Flopsy-Ears' leg.

He twirled and with his other leg, rabbit-stomped me in the face several times.

I winced, but held firm. For a bunny filled with fluff, he sure hit hard.

"Devin!" Mom said. "What are you doing? Get off of me! Get up now!"

"No! I got him! I—"

Me. Flopsy-Ears chomped down on my wrist.

"OW!" I let go, watching helplessly as his fluffy tail hopped away. "Come back!" I scrambled to my feet, but Mom beat me to it.

She blocked my path and grabbed my shoulder. "Devin!"

"But Mom!" I pointed. "He's getting away!"

"Who is?" She turned, but it was too late. Mr. Flopsy-Ears was gone. She glared into my eyes. "I don't know what's going on, but this has to stop."

"The Cuddle Bunny was right there! He bit me! Look, I'll prove it to you!" I rolled up my sleeve to reveal—nothing. "Okay, it didn't go through my clothes, but follow me, and I'll show you!"

She stepped in front of me. "We aren't going anywhere." She turned to Herb. "Herb, I'm sorry about this." She pointed to the overturned chair on the ground. "I'm so embarrassed. I don't know what to say. Devin, apologize to Herb."

"Are you kidding me?"

Herb arched his eyebrows and tilted his head slightly. "Oh, no apology necessary."

"No," Mom said and swatted my shoulder. "Say you're sorry."

I folded my arms against my chest. "Sorry."

"Oh, that's okay, Devin. I'm just glad I was here, as a friend, so I know what needs to be done."

"What do you suggest, Herb?" Mom asked.

"Well, right now, it's obvious to me that Devin is what we in the in the field call coo-coo."

Mom gasped. "Oh, no."

Herb waved her off. "I'm just kidding. There is no real diagnosis of coo-coo. But seriously, for now at least, we have to take everything he says with a grain of salt. His visions might not be accurate and instead be a manifestation of another, deeper issue. A mother's love, perhaps. Maybe, jealousy over a sibling."

"I'm not jealous of Abby."

"Shhh!" Mom held her finger to her lips. "Let Herb speak. Go on, Herb."

"If that's the case," Herb continued, "I'm afraid that not even the great Dr. Sockmund Freud can help. So, what I recommend is keeping him close. Showing him your love. And—" He looked at me. "For right now, taking anything he says with a grain of salt."

The light-bulb finally went off. Herb set me up. This whole thing was done to make me look silly in front of Mom.

"Do you think he should come back?" Mom asked.

"No!" Herb responded quickly. "Er, at least not right now. I think my house upset him today. I suggest keeping poor Devin far away from here for the time being, and then getting lots of rest, so he can begin the slow road to recovery."

"Okay, Herb." Mom nodded. "I'll watch him and keep you updated."

Herb tousled my hair as I flinched. "Good. You just concentrate on getting better."

"There's nothing wrong with me!" I said.

"Come, Devin." Mom took my hand. "Let's get you home."

"No. I'm not going anywhere until you come with me to the other room."

"Devin," Mom said through gritted teeth. "We are going home now."

"But—"

Caw-Caw! Caw-Caw!

I winced. Tommy. I had forgotten all about him.

"On second thought, let's go." I grabbed her wrist and pulled.

"What was that?" Mom asked. "It sounds like a bird."

Herb's eyebrows furrowed. "I don't have a bird."

"That's strange," Mom said. "It sounded like it was coming from right in the house."

"Yes." Herb eyed me. "Yes, it did."

"Mom, let's go now." I dragged her out of the room, up the stairs, and into the darkened hallway.

Herb followed.

I noticed a sliver of light by the door.

I gulped. Tommy had left it open.

I looked back into the house. I wasn't sure what the signal meant—whether he was leaving or just arriving.

I backed toward the door.

A hiss near me. I jumped away. I saw two eyes shining, piercing the darkness. I froze.

"Oh, for heaven's sake, Devin," Mom said. "Stop being afraid, it's just a cat." She opened the door.

The cat turned toward Herb and nodded.

Herb's eyes narrowed. He herded us out the doorway. I felt Dr. Sockmund's cigar push against my back.

"Thanks again, Herb," Mom said.

"My pleasure." Herb smiled, but it wasn't as wide as before. "TTFN. Ta-ta for now." He slammed the door without waiting for a reply.

"That was strange." Mom shrugged. "I can't say that I blame him after all that happened." She grabbed my hand. "Well, let's get you home and maybe some ice cream for my big boy. Remember, Mommy loves you."

The snow had piled up since we had been inside. We trudged across the street. I glanced back and forth between my house and Herb's and wondered if I was going to see Tommy, or if I had just abandoned him to the warlock's den.

CHAPTER TWELVE

DISCOVERIES

The air was chilled and my breath left a vapor trail behind me as I looked back toward Herb's house for any glimpse of Tommy, but there was no sign of him.

"What do you keep looking back for?" Mom asked. "At first I couldn't get you to go to Herb's and now I can't get you to go home? What's with you?"

A million Mom-scenarios went through my mind. I wondered what her reaction would be if I told her that Tommy had broken into Herb's house to snoop while I had kept him busy during my therapy session. They ranged from disbelief and skepticism to the sheer menacing display of her Mom-fury. Whichever reaction it wound up being, I knew one thing: None of them would be good for me.

I decided to keep quiet. I mean, I honestly had no idea if Tommy was in Herb's house or not, but I couldn't afford to wait too long to find out. Either way, I needed to figure this out and fast.

Mom dragged me along up the porch stairs and opened the door to our house. Inside, a trail of long green pine needles led across the floor of the hallway and into the living room. Mom and I glanced at each other and followed them in.

Dad was in the middle of the room, propping up a Christmas tree. Abby was busy on the side rifling through a box labeled ORNAMENTS.

Dad saw us and waved. "Oh, there you are. How'd it go?"

"It was stupid," I said. "Herb had this sock and—"

"That's great!" Dad said. "What do you think of the tree I got? Isn't it fantastic?"

Mom rolled her eyes. "Yes, it's amazing. And it would've been a lot more amazing if we got it a few weeks ago, instead of only a couple of days before Christmas."

Dad wagged his finger. "That's exactly what they want you to do. Do you know what the markup on these things is? When I was installing the water recycling system at the mall, I found out from some of the store owners how much profit they make on retail, and it's absurd. They're a lot more reasonably priced the closer we get to the actual day." He smiled. "They're not used to dealing with someone like me."

Mom sighed. "That's for sure."

Dad motioned me over. "Devin, get over here and give us a hand."

"I still can't find him!" Abby shrieked. "He isn't anywhere!" Her head swiveled in my direction. She zeroed in on me. Her eyes turned blood red. Her nostrils flared and smoke drifted out. She bared her fangs, stuck out her forked tongue, and hissed . . .

Okay, the last part didn't really happen, but it seemed like it could have. For such a little girl, she was seriously creepy at times, and I'm ashamed to say how scared of her I was. I gulped and took a step back.

"You took him!" Abby hissed. "You took Mr. Flopsy-Ears."

"I didn't take him!" I said. "I told you. He hopped across the street to Herb's house. He almost killed Mom and even now, Tommy's a prisoner over there and is probably being tortured as we speak!"

"What?" Dad said.

Everyone looked at me like I was nuts. I wasn't sure I wasn't.

"Oh," Mom said. She glanced at me and then turned back to Dad. "I almost forgot. This is what Herb was just talking about. He says that Devin needs reaffirmation of our love." She motioned with her head toward me, but spoke to Dad. "Tell Devin that you love him."

"What?" Dad seemed confused.

Mom glared at him.

"Tell him!" Mom said.

"Okaaaay." Dad stretched out the word. "We love you, Devin."

"I don't!" Abby chimed in.

"This is ridiculous!" I said. "There's nothing wrong with me."

A rustling sound from within the Christmas tree.

The branches parted.

I jumped back.

A head popped out.

My jaw dropped. "Tommy?"

Dad nodded. "Yeah, what are you talking about him being a prisoner for? He's right here helping me with the Christmas tree."

I stared at Tommy. "How long have you been here?"

Tommy shrugged. "I don't know. A little bit?"

Mom and Dad glanced at each other and then turned to me. This was all I needed. More reasons for them to think I was nuts. I pointed back over my shoulder. "I was just kidding about him being a prisoner at Herb's house. I knew he was here. It was a joke."

Dad shook his head. "I don't get it."

"Never mind," I said. "It's just something the kids at school do now. You know, they say someone is being held prisoner to see reactions. It's just something funny we do."

"No, they don't!" Abby said. "He's lying. Nobody at school does that."

I glared at her. "You don't know what everyone in middle school does."

She crossed her arms in front of her. "I know they don't do that."

I gritted my teeth. "Shut up, Abby."

"Mom!" Abby said.

"Devin!"

"Dad?" I looked at him pleadingly.

He pointed to the tree. "Is anybody going to help me with this?"

Mom rushed over to him. "I'll help you. Everybody else go up to your rooms."

"Going." I didn't want to give her a chance to change her mind. I grabbed Tommy's shirt and yanked him from the tree, pulling him out of the room.

Abby stomped her foot. "But what about Mr. Flopsy-Ears?"

I didn't wait to see what Mom said about the stupid rabbit, and instead dragged Tommy along up the stairs and didn't stop until we reached my room.

"Ow!" He pulled my hand off. "What are you doing? I could've walked myself, you know."

I peeked out into the hallway to make sure nobody was there and then closed the door behind me. I turned to Tommy. He had this clueless look on his face, like he had no idea why I was annoyed. Actually, to be fair, it was pretty much the same look he always had.

"What's the matter with you?" I said.

His brow furrowed. "With what?"

"With what?" I pointed out the window. "I thought you were still at Herb's house."

Tommy cocked his head. "Why would you think that?"

"Because, Tommy, the plan was that I keep him busy while you go there and find stuff out. And I didn't see you, so I thought he captured you."

Tommy aimed his thumbs at his chest. "Shadow, remember. Nobody catches me. I'm too fast. I'm like a ninja, always one step ahead. I had it all worked out. I even told you I was done. Didn't you hear the caw-caw?"

"Yeah, I heard it. But I couldn't find you after. Why do you think I'm asking?"

"Well, as soon as you went in with your mom, I waited like ten minutes before I went over. You know, just to make sure Herb was occupied." He tapped his forehead. "I'm always thinking."

"Yeah, you're a genius. Go on."

"So anyway, I went over and the door was unlocked just like we planned." He nodded at me. "Good job on that."

"Uh, yeah. I took care of it like you asked. Now tell me the rest of the story."

"Okay, so I go in and start looking around, but then remembered, I had no idea what it was that I was looking for. So, I just start walking around and searching through things until I get to the kitchen and that's when I remembered something else."

"What?"

"Your mom never made us breakfast before you left."

"So?"

"So? So, my stomach starts rumbling like really bad, but I figure I'm in the kitchen already, so I start checking out Herb's fridge."

"You went through his fridge?"

He nodded. "I just told you I was hungry. Weren't you listening?"

I slapped my hand over my eyes. "I seriously don't believe you."

"What part of 'I was hungry' weren't you getting? If your mom had made us breakfast, I wouldn't have been."

I felt a pounding behind my eye. "Do twelve-year-old kids get strokes, because I think I'm getting one."

He shook his head. "You're not, you wouldn't be acting so coherent if you were."

I rubbed my temples. My usual Tommy headache was coming on. "I know I'm not getting a stroke, Tommy." I clenched my fists. "Whatever, just go on with the story."

"I'm trying to, but you keep interrupting. So, where was I? Oh, yeah, Herb's house. He didn't have too much, only some bread and cold cuts really. So I made myself a sandwich."

"Of course you would." I groaned. "Can you please get back to the main part? I mean, did you find anything at all or just go there to eat?"

"I'm getting to it! Wow, you're impatient. So anyway, after I made myself the sandwich, I sat down at the kitchen table."

"I think most kids have normal cousins, right? So, why do I get stuck with a moron?"

"Oh, yeah?" Tommy smirked. "Well, would a moron get these?" He reached into his pocket, fished something out, and opened his hand.

"Ketchup packets?"

"Oh, sorry." He shoved them back into his pocket and reached into the one on the other side. "I meant these!" He held out a couple of envelopes. "Letters. They were all over his table."

I reached out for them. "What are they?"

"They're all from the FAB Corporation."

"FAB? Why is FAB writing to Herb?"

"Read 'em. I took a couple, but there were a lot more. All of them saying pretty much the same thing. Herb pitching them some idea and them turning him down. Each and every time."

I opened one of the envelopes and pulled out a letter and unfolded it. It was a printed reply, with Herb's previous correspondence included.

```
Dear Mr. Dorfman,
While we do appreciate the level of
persistence you have shown, we regret
to inform you, for the twentieth
```

time, that we just don't see a match
for your idea within our company.
While we are always searching for
new opportunities here at FABCorp, we
don't feel that your proposal merits
pursuing, as we aspire to much more
grandiose plans than we feel your
idea is presently capable of.

We do wish you the best of luck and
feel free to submit other ideas in
the future.

Sincerely,

J. Sweeney

FABCorp

I put the letter back in the envelope. "I don't get it. What does this have to do with anything?"

Tommy shrugged. "I'm not sure, but like I told you, there were a lot of them. I mean, can you believe how dumb Herb is? Trying for the same thing over and over again? Like, get the hint already. They don't want you."

I looked over the letters again. "I don't know. There has to be more to it. Is that all you found?"

He nodded. "That was it. I didn't have much time. I was reading through them when suddenly I heard this meowing sound. I turned around and saw that creepy cat standing right there in the doorway. That thing was scary.

It hissed at me, so I just grabbed the first two I saw and bolted. That's when I cawed, but it ran after me, so I just ran out the door as fast as I could."

"You didn't look anywhere else?"

"What do you want from me? I got the letters, didn't I? That's more than we had before. I didn't see you doing anything."

"Me? Are you kidding? I'm the one who went down there and had to sit with Herb and Dr. Sockmund!"

Tommy tilted his head. "Who?"

"Dr. Sockmund Freud. It was a sock on his hand that Herb and my mom made me talk to."

Tommy thought a second. "He's probably not a real doctor."

"He's a sock, of course I know he's not a real doctor! That's what I'm telling you. And right in the middle of it all, Mr. Flopsy-Ears appeared and beat me up."

"Really? And your mom didn't do anything?"

I frowned. "She didn't see."

"What do you mean, wasn't she with you? How did she not see?"

"It's complicated. The question is, what do we do now?"

Someone knocked on the door.

Tommy and I looked at each other.

"Yeah?" I called out.

The door opened and Dad popped his head in. "Devin, I have to ask you . . . that whole bunny thing? Is that for real, or a thing you and your school friends are doing?"

"What are you talking about?" I asked.

"C'mon, just like you said about the being taken prisoner thing. I know what's going on. All of you agree to joke about it at once and fool all the grown-ups. Yes, it's very funny. Let's make fun of the adults. I got it."

I glanced at Tommy before turning back to Dad. "I really don't know what you're talking about."

"C'mon, Devin, stop kidding around. I know what you guys are up to. It's all over the news."

"The news?"

"Okay," he sighed. "Don't tell me. But just so you know . . . I know." He popped back out and closed the door.

"What's he talking about?" Tommy asked.

"I don't know. Turn on the TV, quick."

Tommy grabbed the remote off my night table and pressed the button. The TV flashed on.

"The news station," I said. "Hurry."

Tommy pushed the buttons and the news came on. A reporter was standing in front of a house. At the bottom of the screen was a banner that read CUDDLE BUNNY OR RAMPAGING RABBIT?

"Hold it!" I yelled. "Turn up the volume."

The bars on the screen rose and the reporter's voice blared through the speaker. "All over town, we have been hearing of similar incidents of stuffed animals, in particular the FAB Corporation's hot new toy, the Cuddle Bunny, performing acts of mischief and vandalism." The reporter smirked, like he wasn't believing his own story. "Right behind me, police were called to investigate reports of a Bunny which was supposedly seen smashing its way out of the house and tampering with a car in the driveway. I spoke earlier with Officer Hernandez of the Gravesend Police Department, who investigated the case."

A film clip appeared on the screen of an older police officer with a mustache. He was also smirking somewhat. The microphone was in front of him.

"So, officer, do we have a bunny problem in Gravesend?"

The officer laughed. "No, I don't think so. We at the station believe this is all a prank. Not that we don't take every call seriously, but with it being so close to Christmas, I have a feeling that a lot of naughty little boys and girls need a scapegoat so they don't get in trouble with Santa. Therefore, we have a lot of Bunny-blaming."

"So we shouldn't run for the hills and barricade ourselves against an army of marauding rabbits?" the reporter deadpanned.

The officer laughed again. "No, I think we'll be all right."

"I hope you're right, Officer." The reporter turned, faced the camera and smiled. "I just hope this isn't some 'hare-brained' scheme that affects the town." He winked. "This is David Williams reporting. Back to you, Bob."

The news anchors, a man and a woman, both with perfect hair and teeth, appeared on the screen.

The guy spoke first. "I'm still groaning, David. Just be careful out there. If it is an evil bunny, you know how fast they multiply."

The woman laughed. "Oh, Bob."

I stopped listening and turned to Tommy. "Okay, this isn't good."

CHAPTER THIRTEEN

DOUBLE TROUBLE

It was December 24th, Christmas Eve morning, and I was still in bed, exhausted. The night couldn't have seemed any longer. I'm not sure how much I slept, but it definitely wasn't a lot. Mostly I had been lying there again, staring up at the ceiling, thinking about everything that had happened. Warlocks, bunnies, and now the letters Tommy had found at Herb's house. There were just too many thoughts running through my mind to really doze off.

Apparently, just guessing by the sounds of the snores, the same problem hadn't affected Tommy. He'd slept like a baby and was now wide awake, pacing the room, while my eyes felt like there were two weights attached, trying to pull them closed.

Mom and Dad had taken Abby out for last-minute Christmas shopping, but I was too tired to go. Besides, I wanted to give them every opportunity to get me a phone without worrying about me being there. Not that they'd take advantage of it, but this was really my last shot.

As it was, I had a feeling that Christmas was going to be horrible. It wasn't even here yet, and I already knew how it was going to go. My gift would probably be more therapy sessions with Herb, which was just about the only thing they could've given me that would've made the usual socks and underwear look great in comparison.

The more I thought about everything, the more depressed I was getting, which in turn made my headache pound. It already felt like it was going to explode. All I wanted to do was sleep. Unfortunately, all Tommy wanted to do was be Tommy, which even on the best of days was never a good thing, but today, it was fast getting on my nerves.

"I think we have to burn him," Tommy said.

"What?"

"Herb. I think we have to set him on fire."

"Are you psychotic? I'm not burning anybody."

"But that's how you kill a warlock. I've been research-ing it."

"That's how you kill anyone!" I said.

He paused a moment. "Yeah, but it especially works on warlocks."

"You're a moron."

"I don't see you coming up with anything."

"I'm thinking."

"Yeah, while you're busy thinking, Herb and Mr. Flopsy-Ears are right across the street making plans!"

"Plans for what?"

Tommy thought a second. "He's a warlock—what kind of plans do you think they make?"

"To turn us into mice and have cats eat us?"

Tommy stared blankly at me. "Do you hear how dumb you sound when you say things like that? You don't play around with warlocks. They're evil. They want to kill us or make us their slaves or even eat us. Maybe all three. They use kids in soup, you know."

"No, they don't."

Tommy nodded. "Yes, they do. Who's the expert here?"

"I don't think there's a right answer to that question."

"Well, unless you come up with a better idea . . ."

I was about to answer when my thoughts were interrupted by a shadow crossing in front the blinds. A shadow with two long ears!

I bolted upright in my bed. "Tommy," I whispered. "He's here."

Tommy turned, but the shadow was gone. "Who is?"

"Mr. Flopsy-Ears. He's here. I just saw his shadow."

The door clicked.

We whirled toward the sound. Nobody there.

"Somebody locked it," I said.

Something scurried across the floor.

"What was that?" Tommy asked.

I looked at him. "You know what it was." My gaze darted across the room, but saw nothing.

"I'm your furry bestie."

That tinny speaker sound. My heart drummed double-time. The Cuddle Bunny. "We have to get out of here."

Tommy nodded. "I'm with you. Let's go."

I eased myself out of the bed and rushed to Tommy's side.

"Never need to test me."

I tried to pick up where the sound was coming from, but all I could hear was my breathing.

"Because one thing will always be true."

"You look toward the window." I pointed. "I got the door."

Tommy and I stood back to back, circling the room. I held my arms out like claws in front of me, waiting to block or catch anything that might jump out.

"No matter where you go . . ."

We scooted back against the wall.

"I will find you."

Out of the corner of my eye, a streak of white.

I felt nauseated as I turned toward it.

There he was. On my night table. Staring back at me . . . the *Cuddle Bunny.*

I tilted my head. Something was different about him. A black smudge on his cheek. It looked like a scar.

A tap on my shoulder.

"Devin," Tommy whispered.

I didn't look back. "Tommy, he's right here."

"I know, that's what I'm trying to tell you. He's right in front of me by the window."

My eyes narrowed. "What?" I spun around to see Tommy was right. There was a Cuddle Bunny sitting on the dresser right by the window. He arched his eyebrows, smirked, and lifted his paw and pointed behind me.

My shoulders sagged. "Oh, no." Too late, I realized I'd taken my eyes off the Cuddle Bunny on my night table. I peeked back over my shoulder to see a white blur hurtling toward me.

The Cuddle Bunny struck, ramming me into the wall with a thud. I slid down and collapsed into a heap on the floor.

The other Bunny did the same to Tommy, sending him crashing down on top of me.

"Get off!" I shoved Tommy away and frantically searched the room. "Where are they? I don't see them."

"We have to get out of here!" Tommy said.

We scrambled for the door, but something snagged my foot, holding me back.

I stretched up for the doorknob, but it was still inches away. I looked back over my shoulder and saw a Cuddle Bunnies holding each of us by the leg. Scarface Bunny held mine.

Tommy and I glanced at each other.

"Uh-oh," I said.

I dug my fingers into the carpet, but it was no use. They dragged us back into the center of the room and leaped into the air toward us. Scarface Bunny swung his foot up. I tried to block it but it was too late. He nailed me in the face with a sickening, clunking sound, sending me spinning away. He hopped back onto my night table and snatched the letters Tommy had stolen from Herb's house and clutched them in his little paws.

"Stop him!" I said.

He leaped toward the window, but I swiped at him, snatching him out of the air. I managed to get a good fistful of his side.

Scarface Bunny grabbed my wrist tight and swung fully around my arm, until he came back around and hammered into my stomach.

I fell back, but not before tearing a thread from his side.

"Eeeeeeeeee," the Cuddle Bunny shrieked and pulled away.

A piece of Bunny-stuffing was all that was left behind in my fingers.

He bounced up and stomped me into the ground and joined the other one. They both waved and leaped through my window, smashing the glass.

"*NO!*" I yelled and jumped to my feet and ran over, looking out through the new, Bunny-shaped holes.

The FABs scampered across the street toward Herb's house, leaving bunny tracks in the snow.

"What do we do now?" Tommy asked. "There were two of them!"

I clenched my fists and gritted my teeth. "I know there were two of them. I was here with you, wasn't I?"

"I don't get it. How did Mr. Flopsy-Ears do that?"

"Neither one of them was Mr. Flopsy-Ears!"

"What do you mean? Of course it was."

The snow started drifting in through the holes in the window, piling up on the sill.

"Neither one had the bent ear. And the faces were different. The one who took the letters had a scar."

"So, Mr. Flopsy-Ears tore, big deal."

"Trust me, I know Mr. Flopsy-Ears, and neither one was him. All the FABs have slightly different features to get kids to buy more than one. And neither one was him."

Tommy looked out the window. "How many of these things are there?"

"Don't you remember the news report? All those stories of Cuddle Bunnies doing things all over town. Now it makes sense. It wasn't just one Bunny doing it, it was many. Herb's gotten more than one Cuddle Bunny to come to life."

Tommy's jaw dropped. "How many do you think there are?"

I looked out the window for several moments before finally speaking. "I don't know, but we have to find out."

"So what do we do now?"

"There's only one thing to do. We have to go back to Herb's."

I don't think I moved from the living room window for hours. I'd been watching Herb's house while Tommy went home to "prepare," whatever that meant. Mom and Dad still weren't home, and it had already gotten dark outside. I'd have to thank them later for leaving me alone all day with some killer stuffed rabbits on the loose. They hadn't even checked on me once. It was okay though; I still wasn't sure what I was going to tell them about my broken window upstairs. A part of me was tempted to not even mention it and see if they noticed, but I had a feeling the piles of snow on the floor from the two rabbit-sized holes in my window might give it away.

The snow was still falling hard, and the light from the streetlamp reflected off the growing piles on the ground. A wasted day and I still needed to get over to Herb's house, where the lights had been going on and off all day, but there had been no sign of either him or the Cuddle Bunnies.

If Tommy didn't get here soon, I was going to have to do this on my own, except I really had no idea what I was supposed to do.

It wasn't like I could go knock on his door and ask him just exactly how many Cuddle Bunnies he'd brought to life. And even if I could, I really didn't want to sit around and have to listen to him explain it. I'm not sure what was worse—having him maybe be a dangerous warlock or listening to his stories.

I glanced at the clock on the wall. I couldn't wait anymore. When Mom and Dad got home, it'd be much tougher to get out. I had to try now. It was already dark enough that I wouldn't be seen by any neighbors, but not so late that Mom would want to know why I was out. It had to be now.

I passed the Christmas tree on my way to the door and eyed the boxes under it. One in particular caught my eye. A small box, covered in green and red wrapping paper. Just large enough to hold exactly what I wanted. A phone. They actually listened this time and bought me a phone.

They got me a phone!

For that moment at least, all thoughts of warlocks, Cuddle Bunnies, Herb, and Tommy left my mind. All I could think about was this phone. I'd been asking for it for so long and it was finally here. In my hands. I flipped the box over several times and knew one thing. There was no way I could wait until tomorrow. I had to see it.

Now.

I took a quick peek at the door, just in case. Nobody. I carefully lifted the tape, trying not to tear the paper.

Slowly, I peeled it back, leaving very little evidence of what I'd done. Almost there . . .

BANG! BANG! BANG!

A pounding on the door.

My hand jerked forward, tearing the paper from the gift.

"Devin!" from outside.

I gritted my teeth. "Tommy!" I ran to the door and flung it open. "What's wrong with you? You just made me rip the—"

"Move!" Before I could finish my sentence, he shoved me inside and slammed the door behind him.

"What's going on? Wait . . . what are you wearing?"

He had on a yellow construction hat with a flashlight duct-taped to the top. On his back, over his dark jacket, were strapped two water bottles. In his hand a Super Soaker water gun.

He held his finger to his lips. "Shhh!" He dropped to the floor and crawled over to the living room window and reached up to close the curtains. He pressed his body to the floor below the window and slithered his way across and did the same on the other side before finally standing up.

"What are you doing?"

He pointed toward the door. "Across the street. Cuddle Bunnies. I saw like five of them."

"Five?"

He nodded. "But that's not the worst part."

"Worse than five Cuddle Bunnies? What else?"

He was still breathing hard. "I think one of them saw me."

"What? How do you know?"

"I think it was when he turned and looked at me that gave it away."

"Are you kidding me? And you came here?"

"What did you want me to do? He turned real quick, and I couldn't get out of the way fast enough."

"I thought you were supposed to be a shadow!"

"It's not my fault! Didn't you just hear me say that there were a lot of them? It was tough to keep track of so many at once."

"Just great! Did they see you come here?"

He shook his head. "I don't think so. I was too fast for them."

"Oh, I'm sure we have absolutely nothing to worry about."

"It's not like they don't know you live here anyway. It's not a secret to them." He leaned in. "But don't worry. This time, we got 'em."

"What are you talking about? And what's all that stuff on you anyway?"

He flashed a grin. The same one he gave me right before we always got in trouble for something. I hated that grin because it never went well afterwards. I already regretted letting him do anything tonight and we hadn't even started.

"This time I got it." He tapped his helmet. "Light for the darkness." He held up his Super Soaker. "Full tank of holy water." He hitched his thumb over his shoulder toward the two plastic water bottles strapped to his back. "And two bottles in reserve. Nothing can go wrong this time."

I sighed. "No, I'm sure this is all going to work out just fine. You know you said you had holy water last time, and all it did was get Herb's pants wet."

"I was wrong last time. This time it's real though. Trust me."

"But I don't."

"I took this to a priest myself. It's going to work."

"Why don't I believe you?"

"Don't worry," Tommy said. "We already know where the Cuddle Bunnies are. Now, all we have to do is go over there and get some video and pictures of them and show it to people. All we need is some proof."

I knew he was right. Without proof, we would just look insane to everybody. I already did to my parents. If I could get video, all that would change. "All right. What do you have to take video with?"

He shook his head. "Nothing. I don't have a phone. Do you?"

I stared down at the box in my hands. In all the excitement, I had totally forgotten about it. The wrapping paper was partially torn, but for now it didn't matter. I tore off the rest and dropped it to the floor. I turned the box over in my hand several times. My heart sank. "No, no, no! Are you kidding me?" I flipped it several more times, examining the box and making sure I was seeing things right. "An iPod? They got me an iPod? Where's my phone?"

"That's okay," Tommy said. "An iPod can take pictures too. Bring it."

"But it's supposed to be under the tree unopened. If they don't see it when they get back, I'll be in big trouble."

"You won't get in trouble. Parents like when you open your gifts ahead of time."

"No, they don't."

"Yes, they do. It shows them you're excited about what they bought you. Trust me."

"I don't, but anyway, don't I have to charge it first?"

"Nah, that's just a myth. They come ready to go. Come on, let's go already. This is a perfect time. We go over, take some video, and come back before anyone even knows we're gone. It'll be easy."

I looked at the door, shoved the iPod in my pocket, and took a deep breath. "Okay, let's go."

CHAPTER FOURTEEN

THEY MULTIPLY LIKE ... WELL, YOU GET THE IDEA

It was dark out and the dim light from the street lamps wasn't much help. There were still too many patches of the street without light. Patches where Bunnies could be lurking. Even in the low light, though, I could see the vapor trail of my breath. It was freezing and that made it difficult to concentrate. I had to stay focused.

With each step, the snow crunched under my feet. We stuck to the shadows until we reached a large tree and hid behind it. We waited a few seconds until we finally got up the courage to take a peek out. Before us were the hedges surrounding Herb's house. A shudder went through me. Even in the night, this place seemed darker than anything else on the street.

"Okay," I whispered. "Where did you see them?"

Tommy pointed to a dark area at the left of Herb's house. There was no light there whatsoever.

"There?" I asked. "How'd you see them all the way over there? It's not close, and it's so dark out."

"Well, I was a lot closer at the time after I cut through his neighbor's yard and through the hedges."

"You cut through the neighbors' yard?"

"Well, that was the only to look through Herb's window."

"You did what? You didn't tell me that you went onto his property!"

"Since when am I on trial over here? I told you, I wanted to check if I could see the Cuddle Bunnies. Call it advanced scouting. You should be thanking me instead of grilling me with so many questions."

"It was one question!"

"We don't have time for this. Now, do you want to see the Cuddle Bunnies or not?"

I looked back over to the dark patch next to Herb's house and swallowed hard. "It's pretty dark."

"That's why I have this, remember?" He tapped the top of his helmet and the flashlight beamed on. "Who's the smart one now?"

"Will you shut that off?" I smacked the top of his helmet and the light went out. "Do you want to let Herb and the whole neighborhood know that we're here?"

"Ow! That hurt!"

"Good. What do you think people are going to think when they see two kids with a flashlight walking around someone's house?"

"That we lost something."

"In somebody else's yard?"

Tommy shrugged. "You're overthinking this."

I shoved him. "Just go."

I followed Tommy into Herb's neighbor's yard and crept along the hedges, trying to stay low and not be seen. We reached a spot where some of the branches had already been broken and shoved to the side.

He pointed. "That's where I went in before."

Tommy pried the branches apart and held them to the side so I could get through. We were now in Herb's yard on the side of his house. Tommy held his finger to his lips and motioned for me to follow.

I could barely make out his face, it was so dark, but I didn't want him to turn on his flashlight. Instead, I followed the shadowy figure in front of me. We went along, hugging the walls of Herb's house, until he came to a stop.

"Where is it?" I asked.

He pointed above him.

I looked up to see a window, but it was dark.

We grabbed the sill and slowly pulled ourselves up to get a peek through it, but I couldn't make out too much inside.

I turned to him. "I thought you said they were here."

"It's not like they stay in the kitchen!" Tommy said. "Do *you* stay in your kitchen all day?"

I pressed my face against the glass, but was only able to make out the refrigerator and a table. I shivered as the cold bit my cheeks and I wondered just how long we'd have to stand out here.

"I'm your furry bestie."

The song!

Tommy and I whirled around, looking in all directions.

"Where's it coming from?" Tommy asked.

"I don't see anything!" I said.

Tommy pointed at my leg. "Your pocket. It's coming from your pocket."

I winced. "The iPod."

"You have the Cuddle Bunny song on your iPod?"

I shook my head. "No, I didn't put it on. My parents must have." I fished the iPod out and clicked it off. The music stopped.

"Why would they put that on?" Tommy asked.

"How should I know? I'm sick of that stupid Cuddle Bunny and that even stupider song."

"Well, you better hope nobody heard it."

"Yeah, I'm sorry the music wasn't as subtle as your flashlight."

"As long as you have it out, get the camera ready."

"For what?" I asked. "An empty kitchen?"

"Well, when they do come, it's not like you can ask them wait for you. You have to be ready."

"Fine." I slid through the apps on the screen.

I was interrupted by some rustling sounds coming from the side.

Tommy and I whipped our heads toward it. Even in the darkness, I could make out the shadows. Many shadows.

"Tommy?" I whispered. "Turn on the light!"

"But you told me not to turn on the light!"

"Turn it on!"

Tommy tapped his helmet, and the light beamed once again.

My jaw dropped.

In front of us were Cuddle Bunnies. Lots and lots of Cuddle Bunnies. Maybe twenty or more. And they were blocking the path between us and the front of the house.

We turned back to the hedges. There was movement. The branches pried apart and two Cuddle Bunnies thrust their heads through and hissed.

"Run!" I screamed and took off with Tommy right behind me.

"Get a picture first!" Tommy said.

I kept going. "You want me to stop and ask them to pose?"

We ran along the side of the house. The light from Tommy's helmet swiveled all over the place, from the ground to the house to the hedges and then finally back in front of us. It made it difficult to see. We weren't helped at all by the snow already piled on the ground, not letting us get any traction. We reached the backyard and skidded to a stop. Our feet gave out from under us, and we slipped, tumbling to the ground and sinking into the snow.

In the yard, approaching us from the other side, were more Cuddle Bunnies. It looked like there were over fifty of them. They had been waiting for us and now we were surrounded and trapped.

Tommy raised the Super Soaker and began firing wildly. "Aaaaaaaaaaah!" He looked like something out of an action movie, except he was shooting stuffed animals.

The stream of water struck a couple of Bunnies and they shrieked. Not only that, they sizzled. It sounded like bacon frying. Smoke rose from their little stuffed bodies.

"I told you it would work!" Tommy said.

I couldn't believe it, but he was right. It *was* working. "Keep firing!"

The Cuddle Bunnies in front of us scampered back to avoid the spray.

Tommy kept going, but there were too many of them. The Bunnies behind us swarmed like a wave over us and snatched the Super Soaker from his hands.

The stuffed animals pinned our arms and legs to the ground and covered our mouths.

A light snapped on, a small yellow bulb over the back door leading to the house. The door opened. A small figure hopped out and onto my chest.

Mr. Flopsy-Ears!

His beady little button eyes narrowed, and his upper lip curled into a snarl.

A shadow appeared in the doorway behind him. I looked past Mr. Flopsy-Ears to see Herb standing there.

He pyramided his fingers and tapped them against each other. "Oh, my. What do we have here?" He walked over and leaned down until his face was only inches from mine. He smiled. "I've been expecting you." He turned to Mr. Flopsy-Ears. "Get them inside."

CHAPTER FIFTEEN

HERB'S PLAN REVEALED

The room was dark, lit only by a small lamp on an end table. I couldn't make out a lot of the details, but it didn't matter. I knew where we were. I'd already been here: downstairs in Herb's basement office where I'd done my therapy session. The only difference was that last time I wasn't tied to a chair with Tommy by my side in the same predicament.

Herb sat back in his chair, sipping a cup of tea. Mr. Flopsy-Ears sat by his side on one armrest, while the creepy black cat sat on the other, both watching us like some furry little bodyguards. A whole bunch of other Cuddle Bunnies surrounded us.

Herb set his teacup down and tapped his fingers against each other in front of his face as he looked us over. I had no idea what he was thinking, and considering our situation, I'm not sure I wanted to. I became aware of the pounding of my heart, which right about then sounded like a horse galloping through my chest.

I took a peek over at Tommy. By the look on his face, he was just as scared as I was, which only made things worse. No matter how annoying Tommy could be, he always at least seemed like he was brave and knew what he was doing. I sure could have used that now.

Herb leaned forward. "I believe this is the part in the story where the bad guy captures the hero and reveals his plot. Believe me, I've watched enough *Murder, She Wrote* to know."

"What?" I said.

Herb ignored the question and continued. "But believe you me, I'm not the bad guy here."

"Obviously," I said. "Because it's always the good guy who kidnaps and ties up kids and brings stuffed animals to life."

He banged the nightstand, sending the tea cup crashing to the floor.

The cat hissed and jumped off Herb's lap.

The Cuddle Bunnies all hopped back.

Herb looked down at the mess and grimaced. "Now see what you made me do. It was my favorite cup too." He picked it up and showed us how the handle had broken away from the mug. He turned the mug so that the writing on it faced us. It read World's Greatest. . .

"That was the beauty of this cup. It could be for anything. Every day I could pretend it was for something else." He sighed. "Anyway, rest assured, I am the good guy!" He pointed at me. "You know those letters you took from my house?"

I glanced at Tommy. "Technically, I'm not the one who stole them."

"Oh, thanks a lot," Tommy said. "You're blaming me?"

"I'm not blaming you, I'm just saying—"

"Boys!" Herb clapped. "We're getting off track here." He motioned for quiet. "Now, let's all settle down, and let me talk, okay?"

Tommy and I stared at each other and nodded.

Herb smiled. "Good. Now I want you to know, I am the good one. It's the FAB toy company who's bad."

"FAB?" I asked.

Herb nodded. "Yes. I used to work there before I became a therapist."

"You worked at a toy company?" I asked. "But aren't you a warlock?"

"So? A warlock has to earn a living too, you know. How do you expect me to feed myself?"

"By eating the brains of children?" Tommy asked.

Herb scrunched up his nose. "The brains of children? Yuck. Who does that?"

"Uh, I don't know," Tommy said. "Hopefully, not you."

"Oh, heavens no. We don't do that. And besides, red meat is so bad for you. Especially children. Filled with fat and sugar. It's like junk food."

As I sat there watching everything, I wasn't sure what bothered me more: the fact that I was being held captive or that if I was going to die, it was going to be at the hands of crazy little stuffed rabbits and a weird, nonsense-talking warlock.

"So, anyway," Herb continued. "While I was working for FAB, that's when they came out with that ridiculous Hugging Hippo—"

"Boooooooo!" the Cuddle Bunnies hissed collectively.

Herb motioned for them to quiet down. "I know. I know. They're terrible, ugly creatures. A hippo? Honestly, who hugs a hippo? People think they're so cute, but they don't realize how dangerous hippos are. Nobody, but nobody should ever be hugging a hippo, let alone a child. It's ludicrous and I told Sweeney that."

"Sweeney?" I asked.

"The president of development at FAB." He sighed. "I wrote her many times, but she just ignored me." He shook his fist in the air. "She rejected every idea and instead pushed forward for a whole line of furry, smiling hippos. I mean, seriously . . . hippos don't even have fur!"

"What does that have to do with anything?" I asked.

"That's what I'm telling you. I told her how ridiculous it was to have a hippo and told her about my idea for a line of adorable, fluffy little bunnies that every child could take care of and hug. More specifically, cuddle."

My eyes widened. "The Cuddle Bunny was *your* idea?"

Herb nodded. "Yep. And do you know what she told me?"

I shook my head. "What?"

"She told me that there was no place in their line for a bunny, but to feel free to send in other toy ideas in the future."

"Wow, that stinks," Tommy said.

"Wait, I'm not done," Herb said. "I knew she was wrong and wrote her back many times, telling her. I mean, who doesn't love a bunny, right? But after the tenth letter, she started getting nasty and told me not to write anymore. After the twentieth letter, she fired me!" His fists clenched and his nostrils flared.

"But"—I looked around the room—"the Cuddle Bunnies were made. They're like everywhere."

Herb gritted his teeth. "Exactly. She stole my idea! The Cuddle Bunnies were mine! She told me my idea was silly, then fired me and stole it."

"Did you write the song too?" Tommy asked.

I looked at him. "Seriously?"

Tommy shrugged. "Why? I think it's kind of catchy."

"Thank you," Herb said. "I'm very proud of it."

I cleared my throat. "I don't understand. If they stole your idea, why'd you bring the Cuddle Bunnies to life?"

"Because"—Herb's voice lowered—"I'm going to ruin them. They stole my Cuddle Bunnies, so I'm going to make the Cuddle Bunnies go on a path of destruction that will leave the FAB toy company in ruins. People everywhere will associate the devastation they saw during Christmas with FAB and never buy another toy from them again." He glanced at his watch. "And that reminds me. It's time."

"Time for what?" I said.

"Time for the furry carnage to begin."

"But wait a second," I said. "What about all the kids who bought Cuddle Bunnies? You're ruining it for them."

"That's a sacrifice that has to be made for now."

Herb rose from his chair and pointed toward the door. "Go forth, my furry friends. It is time to wreak havoc, cause chaos, and ruin the FAB name forever!"

A high-pitched Bunny shriek rose from the mass of Cuddle Bunnies and they swarmed out the door. A mob of furry vengeance. They flooded out of the room and up the stairs.

I heard the sound of their little paws scampering through the house. After a few minutes there was silence.

The cat purred and rubbed itself against Herb's leg.

"What are they going to do?" I said.

Herb sat back down and smiled. "Don't worry, I won't let it go on for too long. A few hours, and then I'll show up and save the day."

"What are you talking about?" I said.

"I'll appear and take care of all the Cuddle Bunnies and everyone will be so grateful to me that they'll do anything I want."

Out of the corner of my eye, I saw Mr. Flopsy-Ears and a couple of the other Cuddle Bunnies appear back at the top of the staircase, but Herb didn't seem to notice.

The cat swiped at Herb's leg and meowed excitedly.

Herb shooed it away. "Not now, Wendigo!"

It gave me an idea. I needed to press this.

"What is it that you want?" I asked.

Herb smiled, sat up in his seat, and reached behind him. He wriggled his arm.

I winced. I already knew what was coming.

Herb turned back toward us with his arm in a sock. Dr. Sockmund Freud. "These will be my new creations."

"Sock puppets?" I asked. "You want to make sock puppets?"

Mr. Flopsy-Ears appeared in the doorway and stared at Dr. Sockmund. Herb was still too focused on us to notice.

"Not just regular sock puppets," Herb said. "A whole line of them. Each one will be in the likeness of a different celebrity."

"That sounds ridiculous," I said.

"What other celebrities?" Tommy asked.

"Well," Herb said. "Different celebrities from different fields like movie stars and musicians, like Clint Sockwood, Johann Sebastian Sock, and Elvis Sockley."

"Nobody's going to want to play with those," I said.

"How much for the Elvis Sockley?" Tommy asked.

I glared at him. "Really?"

Tommy shrugged. "What? I'm just curious."

"But these won't be just any regular sock puppets. They'll also be animated. Besides knowing all the information about the person they're named after, they will be sentient toys. They'll sing and have interactions with the child. They'll be educational and fun."

"Can you save an Elvis Sockley for me when you're done?" Tommy said.

Behind Herb, Mr. Flopsy-Ears appeared with the other two Cuddle Bunnies.

"How will you get the sock puppets to come to life?" I asked.

"Same way I got the Cuddle Bunnies. I still have some potion saved. I didn't give everything to Mr. Flopsy-Ears."

I took a quick peek over at Mr. Flopsy-Ears. Maybe, if I could keep Herb talking, the Cuddle Bunnies and Herb would distract each other until I could figure out a way for Tommy and me to escape. "You gave Mr. Flopsy-Ears a potion?"

"Of course." Herb laughed. "He was the instrument of my revenge. He went all over town bringing Cuddle Bunnies to life, so they could do my bidding."

"What happens to the Cuddle Bunnies now?" I asked.

"That's easy," Herb said. "Once their task is completed, I'll just reverse the spell and revert them into harmless stuffed animals again. Everyone will thank me, I'll be a hero, and toy companies everywhere will be fighting each other to produce my sock puppets." He gazed off like he was dreaming. "Finally, the world will recognize the genius of Herbert T. Dorfman."

"That sounds great." I nodded. "The FAB Corporation was wrong. I hope you give them what they deserve. Now, can you let us go? My parents should be home any minute now, and I don't want to get in trouble for being out."

Herb laughed. "I can't let you go."

I gulped. "Why not? I won't tell anyone, I promise. I just told you I think the FAB Corporation deserves this."

"Nice try," Herb said. "But I need you both to stay here until my work is done."

"A-and then what?" My voice quivered.

Herb's eyes narrowed. "And then you will be taken care of."

"I knew it!" Tommy shouted. "He's going to turn us into zombie slaves."

"Oh, heavens no." Herb snorted. "Zombies are such a pain. Very complicated to create and then in the end much more trouble than they're worth. I think a simple memory-wipe will do, although I'm not sure I have all the proper ingredients." He shrugged. "Oh well. I'll figure it out and then send you both on your way. But first this needs to be—"

A loud thunking sound interrupted him.

Herb's eyes rolled up into his head. He slumped over and fell off the chair to the ground. Behind him stood Mr. Flopsy-Ears. He was holding a trophy in his hand. Even from here, I could make out the words HONORABLE MENTION on it. The other two Cuddle Bunnies hopped up on either side of Mr. Flopsy-Ears. One was Scarface Bunny, the one I pulled a piece of fluff from, but the other one I didn't recognize.

From the side of the room, a black blur shot out and skidded to a halt in front of the Cuddle Bunnies. It was Wendigo, Herb's cat. It hissed at the Bunnies and arched its back, its fur rising. I was briefly aware of how embarrassing it was to be rescued from a bunch of stuffed animals by a cat, but I couldn't afford to be choosy now. Hopefully, this cat was as fierce as he was scary.

The Cuddle Bunnies stared at Herb's cat, then looked at each other. They shrugged and turned back to Wendigo, lifted their paws, and hissed back.

Wendigo whimpered a soft meow and scurried from the room.

Well, so much for that. Stupid cat. That's why I was a dog person anyway.

With the cat gone, the three Cuddle Bunnies turned their attention back toward us.

I tried to get up and run, but remembered I was tied to the chair.

"Devin?" Tommy whispered.

"Yeah?"

The Cuddle Bunnies took a step closer.

"What are we going to do now?

"I have no idea."

Their eyes narrowed. They snarled . . . and leaped straight at us.

CHAPTER SIXTEEN

CODE BREAKERS

As the Cuddle Bunnies hurtled toward us, I realized there was nowhere for me to go. Their feet were aimed straight for my face and I was tied to a chair, so I did the only thing I could think of and heaved my body back. The chair toppled and landed with a crash. The wood from the backrest splintered and broke away from the seat as a Cuddle Bunny sailed overhead.

I tugged at the ropes.

Thankfully, they were now loose enough for me to wrench from the chair, allowing me to slip my feet out and scramble away. But before I could get too far, the Bunnies were on me.

One jumped on my shoulders and grabbed my hair like the reins of a horse.

"Ow!" I yelled, reaching back to try to get him off. Unfortunately, this kept me too preoccupied to see another one rocket into my stomach. "*Oof!*" I doubled over.

"Will you stop fooling around?" Tommy said. "Get me out of this!"

Even if I wanted to answer him, I couldn't. The Bunny had knocked all the air out of me.

I whirled and swung wildly, hoping to just hit something, anything, when my fist finally connected.

A Bunny shriek followed by the sound of smashing glass. I had knocked a Bunny into one of the pictures on the wall, breaking the frame. I glanced up at the one on my shoulder and saw it was Scarface Bunny. He looked stunned by the scene. I used the opportunity to reach up and grab him by the arm.

He chomped down on my hand.

"OW!" These things were starting to hurt more and more. Rage bubbled inside me. I flung him into the wall next to the other one. Two of them down, but I knew it wouldn't be for long. That left only—

In the corner of my eye, a movement.

"Watch out!" Tommy yelled.

I swerved just in time to avoid the trophy that whizzed by my head. I turned to the direction it came from to see . . .

Mr. Flopsy-Ears.

I scanned the room quickly, searching for anything to use as a weapon. Another sound to the side. The other two Cuddle Bunnies were starting to stir. This had to be fast.

Mr. Flopsy-Ears picked up the tea cup from Herb's end table and threw it at me.

I ducked and dropped to the floor and there I saw it. Behind the couch. Tommy's Super Soaker filled with holy water.

Mr. Flopsy-Ears followed my gaze.

We looked each other in the eyes, just for a moment, before we made a mad dash toward the Super Soaker.

"What are you doing?" Tommy yelled.

I dove across the floor, reaching for the Super Soaker at the same time as Mr. Flopsy-Ears arrived. I grabbed one end while he grabbed the other.

He used his end to swing around and nail me in the chin with his foot. I saw stars for a second, but held tight. No way was I letting go. This was my only shot.

I balled my other hand into a fist, gritted my teeth, and with everything I had, reached back and hammered into Mr. Flopsy-Ears' side.

He winced.

I'd hurt him, but the pain didn't seem to last too long. Maybe a few seconds, tops. He turned to me. His eyes narrowed, and his lip raised into a snarl. A low growl rumbled up from inside him.

Only one thought went through my mind. *Uh-oh.*

Mr. Flopsy-Ears pounced. His little paws delivered blow after blow to my body.

I tried to shield myself as best as I could while still clinging to the Super Soaker, but I was in pain. I moved my fingertips over it until I felt the trigger and pulled. A stream of holy water shot out. From my vantage point on the floor, I couldn't even see where it landed, but I heard the yelp, followed shortly by a sizzling sound.

Mr. Flopsy-Ears and I turned toward it. I'd blindly struck Scarface Bunny, who was clutching his shoulder. A stream of smoke hissed into the air from his wound.

Using the distraction, I grabbed Mr. Flopsy-Ears by his tail. He spun toward me. His eyes flashed with murder, but before he could react I hurled him across the room.

I gripped the Super Soaker tightly and aimed it at the now regrouped trio of Cuddle Bunnies. "Stay back, Mr. Flopsy-Ears! I'm warning you."

Mr. Flopsy-Ears shielded his mouth from me and whispered something to the other two. Their ears wriggled and they nodded. They fanned out across the perimeter of the room. Mr. Flopsy-Ears and Scarface Bunny went one way, and the third Bunny went the other.

I swiveled from side to side.

"Shoot them!" Tommy said. "What are you waiting for?"

I fired wildly. Twisting back and forth between the Cuddle Bunnies, just hoping to strike anything. But they were faster. They jumped, hopped, and scurried to avoid the spray.

"Will you stop playing around?" Tommy said. "Hit them."

"What do you think I'm trying to do?" I asked.

I fired at anything that moved, narrowly missing each time, until—

"Eeeep!" Another yelp, followed by more sizzling and a swirl of smoke.

I'd hit the nameless Bunny. He'd dropped to the ground. I didn't hesitate and fired again, drenching him in holy water. Smoke filled the air.

A growl from the side. I turned.

Scarface Bunny glared at me. He snarled and bared his teeth.

I aimed the Super Soaker.

A whistling behind us. We spun toward it.

Mr. Flopsy-Ears was standing by the foot of the staircase. He motioned for Scarface Bunny.

Only one problem—I was between them.

Scarface Bunny charged straight toward me and leaped.

I fell back, but lifted the Super Soaker and fired. The spray missed as Scarface Bunny sailed over. I turned just in time to see him and Mr. Flopsy-Ears bounding up the steps. I thought briefly about following, but quickly realized I really didn't want to catch up to them yet. At least not alone.

"Okay, can you get me out now?" Tommy shouted as if reading my mind.

I ran over to him. "Sorry, but I was kind of busy." I put the Super Soaker down and untied him.

Tommy rubbed his wrists where the rope had been. He pointed. "Wow, look at that."

The Bunny I had hit with the holy water was now a mass of twitching liquid fur and goo.

"That is so cool!" Tommy said. "A Puddle Bunny."

"Gross." I wrinkled my nose. "How did that happen?"

"I told you," Tommy said. "Because they're magic. Evil magic. And that's what holy water does to dark magic." He picked up the Super Soaker. "Now, all we have to do is get the rest of them."

"Oh, is that all? Did you see how fast they moved? We don't have enough holy water here, and there were, like, fifty of them."

"More . . ." A groan from the center of the room.

Tommy and I followed the direction of the voice.

There, struggling to sit up and rubbing the back of his head, was Herb.

We walked over slowly. Tommy raised the Super Soaker.

"What are you talking about?" I asked.

Herb dragged himself to a wall and leaned back against it. He held one hand pressed against the back of his head. His eyes were closed. His breathing slow. "There are going to be more than fifty of them. Way more."

"How?" I asked. "You're the one who brought them to life and you're here."

Herb shook his head. "I did bring them to life, but it was the potion I made. Mr. Flopsy-Ears took it with him. All it takes is a drop to animate them."

"Where are they going?" I asked.

Herb didn't answer. His chest rose and fell several times.

"Hello?" Tommy said. "Herb?"

"Sorry," Herb said. "I think I need a doctor."

"Where are they going?" I asked.

"First to the mall. There's a secret shipment of Cuddle Bunnies coming in. Last minute for Christmas Eve."

"What do you mean by first?" I asked. "You said 'first to the mall.' Where are they going after?"

Herb took a deep breath. "To the FAB factory."

Tommy and I exchanged looks.

"It's about a mile out of town," Herb said. "If they get there . . ."

"Herb, how do we stop them?" I asked.

"There's only one way. I have a reverse potion. You have to use it on them."

"Where is it?" I shouted.

"In my safe."

"Where's your safe, Herb?" I said.

Herb lifted his arm.

A stream of water sprayed his face.

I turned to Tommy. "What are you doing?"

He shrugged. "Sorry, I thought he was making a move."

I swatted the Super Soaker down. "Will you put that thing away?"

Tommy stared at Herb. "Wait a second. Why isn't he burning?"

I also examined Herb. "Yeah, why aren't you burning?"

"Because, you imbeciles, holy water only works on evil. I'm not evil, I'm merely disgruntled. The Cuddle Bunnies are evil. Now, will you please get me a doctor?"

"Where's the safe?" Tommy asked.

Herb sighed and raised his arm again. "It's right over . . ." His arm dropped and he slumped over.

"Herb?" I called out. He didn't move. "Herb?"

Tommy reached out with the Super Soaker and nudged Herb with it. Still nothing. "I think we killed him."

"No, look." I pointed. Herb's chest rose and fell slowly. "He's still breathing."

By the time I finished my sentence, Tommy wasn't even near me anymore. He was already busy looking behind a pillow on the couch. "Huh? Oh, yeah. That's good. Now, help me find that safe." He continued searching the room. "It's got to be in here somewhere."

"What about Herb?" I asked. "Shouldn't we call the police and get him an ambulance?"

Tommy glanced at Herb. "I guess." He dragged out the word. "But the safe first."

"But what if he dies?"

"He's not going to die. You're so dramatic. He just got hit on the head. People get hit on the head all the time in the movies and they're fine."

"This isn't the movies!"

"Same thing. Now, think a second. What if the police come and ask what we're doing here? You going to tell them that we got kidnapped by a bunch of stuffed animals? They'll never believe it and then we'll never find the safe and the Cuddle Bunnies will just cause mayhem all over town. And if they reach that factory, forget about it. Who knows what they'll do?" Tommy shook his head. "We have to find that safe now. It's our only chance. Then, right before we leave, we can call the police."

I thought a moment and looked at Herb. He looked really hurt, but he was breathing okay. And besides, Tommy was right. We couldn't have the police ask too many questions. They'd never believe us anyway and we needed that reverse potion. We had to find it before we did anything else. I nodded. "Okay, where do you think it is?"

"How should I know? Just start looking everywhere, but hurry. We don't have much time."

Tommy and I rummaged through the room, searching behind the couches and through the desk.

After around ten minutes of finding nothing, I stopped and looked around the room at all the paintings. My eyes came to rest on one of an old balding guy in a suit. He was holding a cigar in one hand. "That one!" I pointed. "He looks like Herb's puppet, Dr. Sockmund Freud."

We moved closer.

I lifted the painting away. "Yes!" I shouted. Behind it was a safe built into the wall. There was no dial on it with numbers like I always saw in the movies. Instead, there was a small electronic screen with seven buttons under it. Below them was a single red button that read SUBMIT.

"Well, what do we do now?" I asked. "We don't know the combination."

"I don't know." Tommy shrugged. "Let's just guess something." He tapped away at the first button and different letters scrolled by on the screen. "Wait a second. Seven letters? Herb?" He smirked. "It's too easy." He punched the buttons until the screen read WARLOCK. He pressed the submit button.

A big red X appeared on the screen, followed by a loud buzzing sound. The screen then read YOU HAVE FOUR TRIES LEFT BEFORE ALL CONTENTS WILL BE DESTROYED.

I swatted his chest. "Great! You just wasted one. Why would he put down warlock?"

"Because he is one, that's why!"

"He wouldn't put that down as a password!"

"How was I supposed to know? I don't see you coming up with anything."

I tapped the screen. "Don't put in anything else yet. We only have four tries left. It has to be something that he likes. Something that means something to him."

Tommy snapped his fingers. "I got it!" He punched the buttons until the screen read SOCKMUN.

"No, don't!" I yelled, but it was too late. Tommy pressed SUBMIT.

Another red X. Another buzz, followed by YOU HAVE THREE TRIES LEFT BEFORE ALL CONTENTS WILL BE DESTROYED.

"Will you stop pressing things?" I yelled. "What's with you? First of all, that's a ridiculous guess and secondly, it would be Sockmund with a 'D' at the end, not Sockmun! There are only seven letters, you can't just force in words." I stared down at the painting I had taken off the wall. "Wait, try Sigmund."

Tommy pressed the buttons again.

Another buzz. Another X. Two tries left.

"Great," Tommy said. "You thought Sockmun was dumb? Well, Sigmund is dumber. Why would he use the same name as the place he's hiding it? It makes no sense."

"It was better than Sockmun!"

Tommy snapped his fingers. "Wait! This time I have it. I promise. I can't believe we didn't think of it before." He typed in a few letters until it read CUDDIEB.

Another X.

"Oops!" Tommy said. "Sorry."

I held my hand up. "Stop! Don't touch a thing. Not a thing! We only have one try left."

"Fine!" Tommy said. "So, what do you think it is?"

"I don't know. Just give me a second." I rubbed my eyes and tried to think. It had to be something he liked. Something special to him. But what? I went over every conversation that Herb and I ever had. The only problem was he had said so many weird things and I didn't understand half of them. I replayed everything he ever said again and again, then something popped into my mind. A conversation we'd had. I counted the letters in my head and looked at the screen. "I think I know." I tapped the buttons. P-I-C-K-L-E-S.

"Pickles?" Tommy asked. "What's Pickles?"

"It's from some stupid TV show that Herb used to like. He said it was his favorite as a kid. I'm trying it." My hand trembled as I reached for the screen. I placed my finger on the red SUBMIT button, closed my eyes, took a deep breath, and pushed.

The screen flashed green. There was a loud click.

The safe door swung open.

CHAPTER SEVENTEEN

BUNNIES RUNNING WILD

I wasn't sure what bothered me more, that we were hunting down over fifty Cuddle Bunnies, or that we were armed with only one thermos-sized bottle of holy water and a small vial of Herb's reverse potion, which had only about an ounce in it.

Tommy held the vial in front of his face. "What are we supposed to do with this?" He pressed down on the cork-stopper at the top and tilted it sideways as the blue liquid sloshed back and forth inside.

"I don't know," I said. "But we can't just stay here."

Screeeeeech! The sounds of tires skidding.

CRASH!

Tommy and I jumped.

"What was that?" I asked.

"It came from outside!' Tommy said. "C'mon, let's go see!" He bounded up the stairs.

"Wait!" I said. "What about Herb?"

"He'll be fine!" Tommy said. "Let's go!"

I glanced at Herb. He was still slumped over, but breathing.

"You're going to be okay," I said and knew how stupid it was since he couldn't hear me anyway, but it seemed like the right thing to do at the time.

I raced up the steps and out the front door. The snow pelted me right away. I walked out a little further, past the hedges. Two guys were yelling at each other in the street. It looked like one of them had crashed into a parked car, which seemed like it belonged to the other one.

Tommy stood nearby, watching.

I walked over to him. "What happened?"

Tommy pointed to them. "Listen."

"I'm telling you," one of the guys said. "It wasn't my fault. A rabbit hopped onto my windshield and blocked my view."

"C'mon," the other guy said. "A rabbit isn't hopping onto a moving car."

"This one did! I swear. And then he—" He closed his mouth and shook his head.

"And then he what?" the second guy asked.

"Well, then he pressed his face against the glass and stuck his tongue out at me."

CRASH!

It came from the next block.

Tommy swatted my arm. "Another one! C'mon!"

He took off and I followed.

We rushed as fast as we could through the snow. By the time we reached the next accident, there were already a bunch of people out on the street. All of them shouting at each other. All about the same thing.

A bunny. A Cuddle Bunny.

Tommy grabbed the sleeve of my coat. "Look."

All the way down at the end of the block, more people were outside milling about and yelling at each other. Another car crash. This time into a pole. We ran closer. Power lines were down with sparks flying. Traffic lights blinked, alternating between red and green every other second. From what I could see, it was the same scene being replayed block after block.

Even if we hadn't already known exactly where the Cuddle Bunnies were going, they were leaving a very clear trail for us to follow.

"It's around half a mile to the mall," Tommy said.

I looked up at the falling snow and then back toward my house. I pulled my coat up around my neck to shield it from the cold. "Let's go."

By the time we got to the mall, I realized two things. First thing, half a mile was a whole lot farther than I thought it was. Especially in the cold and snow. The wind was biting my hands and face. My fingers were numb, and I couldn't feel my toes. I had no idea how Tommy walked all that way holding the Super Soaker.

The other thing I noticed?

The path of destruction the Cuddle Bunnies had created around the neighborhood had all but disappeared by the time we reached the mall. Here it was silent. Almost too silent. The only sound that really stood out was the wind whistling by. The lot was packed, but all of the cars seemed intact. As far as I could tell, nothing had been done to any of them, and for some reason that scared me even more.

"I don't see any sign of them," I said.

Tommy shrugged. "Maybe we beat them here?"

"There's no way we beat them here."

"How do you know? We were walking pretty fast."

"Because they're rabbits! They're faster than us." I looked around the parking lot. "They have to be here somewhere."

Tommy raised the Super Soaker and swiveled between cars. "Yeah, but the trick is finding them. They could be anywhere."

We threaded our way through the lot, stopping at every sound. Looking around every car, just in case anything hopped out at us. By the time we reached the front of the mall, I was already winded from stress. These Cuddle Bunnies were making me a wreck.

We arrived at the glass doors that led into the mall.

"See?" Tommy said. "Nothing. I told you we beat them here."

At that moment, somebody screamed. Through the glass doors, a swarm of people all running toward us. The mall doors burst open, and crowds came spilling out.

"Run for your lives!" someone shouted. "They're all over the place!"

I turned to Tommy. "I think we found them."

The mob of people stampeded past without seeming to notice us. I worried about being trampled, but worried even more about how stupid we were to be running toward something that everybody else was running from.

We wove through the onrushing crowd until we got inside. There was only one word to describe what I saw in front of me: chaos. People were running in every direction, but mostly out.

"It's the Most Wonderful Time of the Year" blared over the mall speakers like nothing at all was wrong. Garbage and shopping bags littered the floor. People had sure left in a hurry. In front of us was a directory board, but I didn't need it. I already knew where we were. Further up and around the corner was the Helen of Toys store. That's where they would be.

"C'mon!" I said.

Tommy and I took off running. I had to admit, as much as he got on my nerves at times, I sure felt better when he was there.

We reached the end of the corridor and stopped by a corner electronics store. It was deserted. No customers and no workers. Anybody could have stolen anything they wanted, but it didn't look like anyone cared too much about that. They were too concerned with getting away from a bunch of marauding bunnies.

We pressed our backs to the wall.

Tommy held his finger to his lips. "I'm going to check if the coast is clear."

I nodded and watched as he swung around with the Super Soaker. The color drained from his face.

He lowered the water gun and came back around to hiding against the wall. "I think we might be in trouble."

"What is it?" I asked.

He stared straight ahead, but it didn't look like he was taking anything in. "Look for yourself."

I edged past Tommy and peered around the corner. My jaw dropped. Cuddle Bunnies were everywhere. To the right, a Cuddle Bunny squirting mustard from a pretzel stand at running children. To the left, another Cuddle Bunny gorging himself on candy, his belly already blowing up like a balloon. Straight past them, on the small electric train for children, Bunnies in the engineer car, pulling the whistle. Everywhere else were broken store windows and Bunnies looting.

A mall cop ran by, covering his eyes and screaming. On his back, a Cuddle Bunny, laughing and pressing down on a canister of pepper spray.

All I wanted to do was run, but didn't know if I could, even if I tried. My feet felt like two slabs of cement, rooted to the spot.

A couple of stores down, a window smashed and a Cuddle Bunny leaped out, covered in diamond necklaces.

Another Cuddle Bunny hopped over and laughed, reaching for one. Jewelry-wearing Cuddle Bunny swatted his paw away. The little thief Cuddle Bunny tried again, but jewelry-wearing Cuddle Bunny reached down and held up a small black device in his paw and then pressed it into thief Cuddle Bunny's side. Thief Cuddly Bunny spasmed several times and collapsed to the ground.

My shoulders sagged. "He tased him."

"What?" Tommy asked.

"They have weapons!" I said. "What do we do now?"

"It doesn't matter what they have." Tommy held up the Super Soaker. "We have this!"

I searched through the pandemonium for the Helen of Toys store and found it midway through the throng. Cuddle Bunny after Cuddle Bunny popped out the front, like the store was spitting them out one at a time.

I pointed. "There's the toy store. We have to get over there."

Tommy nodded. "Okay, you go. I'll cover you."

"What do you mean, you'll cover me? Why don't I cover you?"

Tommy held up the Super Soaker. "Duh, because I'm the one holding the gun."

"I'm not going unless you're coming with me."

"What? That's silly, how is that covering you then?"

"I don't care if you cover me or not. You're coming. I'm not going alone."

He rolled his eyes and sighed. "Fine. Okay, on the count of three."

I eyed him up and down. "Okay, on three. One . . ."

"Two," Tommy said.

"Three!" I jumped out into the open and ran several yards before I realized that Tommy wasn't with me. "Darn it, Tommy!"

"Go!" Tommy said. "I'm covering you!"

I raced through the mayhem. The Cuddle Bunnies seemed too busy looting and destroying to pay any attention to me. To them, I was just another person running. I kept going until I reached the toy store and ducked inside. At the front, leaning to the side, was a sign attached to a metal post:

CUDDLE BUNNIES
NOW IN STOCK!
(WE ALSO HAVE HUGGING HIPPOS!)

The store was deserted. It looked like a hurricane had torn through. Almost everything was off the shelves and scattered across the floor. The only thing in the store left in place were Hugging Hippo boxes. Shelf after shelf lined with them. I looked at the sign next to them.

HUGGING HIPPOS NOW MARKED DOWN 50%!

"Nobody wants the stupid Hugging Hippos," I said.

Some scuffling noises came from the back.

I crept down the aisle toward it. The store speakers blared "Silent Night," yet there was nothing quiet about the way my heart was pounding. I was convinced you could hear it over the music. Even my breathing was loud. I needed to calm down if I hoped to get out of this in one piece.

I reached the end of the aisle and peered around. Cuddle Bunny boxes were everywhere, but mostly in a big pile in the corner. There must have been around fifty or sixty of them. All of them ripped open and empty. Off to the side stood a big brute of a Cuddle Bunny hovering over a box.

"Oh no," I muttered. "The Cuddle Bunny Deluxe."

The Cuddle Bunny Deluxe was a three-foot-tall, limited-edition variant. Only one hundred of them in the country. Two per state. Lucky me that this store had one of them.

I had never seen one in person. The only thing I could say about it was that I was sure the FAB Corporation had no idea just how dangerous it would be if it ever came to life. He had hunched shoulders and large, protruding bunny teeth. His ears were long; his eyes seemed dull and unintelligent. He was a hulking brute. And he was the one I had to stop.

He tore open a smaller Cuddle Bunny box and yanked the stuffed animal free from the plastic ties. He reached out. In his paw, he had an eyedropper filled with some red liquid. Cuddle Bunny Deluxe held it over the lifeless toy and squeezed. A small red drop dripped out and landed on the smaller Bunny's nose.

Instantly, the smaller Bunny threw his head back like he had been jolted by a surge of electricity. He trembled and shook, like he was working on a jackhammer. A small popping sound and the Cuddle Bunny sprang into the air, throwing its arms and legs out to the side. It landed on its feet and nodded up at Cuddle Bunny Deluxe.

"No way!" I said and took a step back. My foot landed on something and I slipped. "Whoa!" I shouted and fell back against the shelves, knocking over some Hugging Hippo boxes. I fell to the ground, landing on my butt.

I looked up to see Cuddle Bunny Deluxe and the newly alive Cuddle Bunny staring back.

CHAPTER EIGHTEEN

CUDDLE BUNNY DELUXE

I backpedaled away from the approaching Cuddle Bunnies until I smacked into the shelves behind me. Several Hugging Hippo boxes toppled down on me.

Cuddle Bunny Deluxe sneered. He had this crazed, murderous look in his eyes. He and his newly created side-kick took another step toward me.

On impulse, I grabbed box after box of Hugging Hippos and heaved them at the Cuddle Bunnies.

Cuddle Bunny Deluxe threw his paws up to block them. A couple rebounded and clunked Sidekick Bunny on the head. Cuddle Bunny Deluxe snickered a moment, until the box hit the floor, triggering the music. That stupid Hugging Hippo song.

I'm a Hugging Hippo
I'm your Hugging friend
We'll always be together

I'll follow you to the end

Both Bunnies recoiled.

Cuddle Bunny Deluxe let go of the eyedropper and yanked his ears down.

His sidekick tore at his own fur.

They hated the Hugging Hippo song. I couldn't say I blamed them. It was the only thing I ever heard that made the Cuddle Bunny song even halfway listenable.

This was my chance. I wasted no time in grabbing more boxes, attacking instead of waiting. I hurled box after box toward them, and with each one that hit, the song went off. With each lyric sung, the Cuddle Bunnies howled.

Cuddle Bunny Deluxe growled and hissed. He clenched his paws, cast a downward glance at his sidekick, and in one swoop scooped him up and launched him at me. Fast. Before I could move, Sidekick Bunny was on me. He grabbed my ears and head-butted me.

I saw black for a moment. Something rammed my side, knocking me back down to the floor. It felt big. I blinked several times. My vision cleared just in time to see Cuddle Bunny Deluxe's massive paw balled into a fist and headed straight at my face. I braced myself for the blow, but suddenly it stopped in midair and opened.

A yelp of pain.

A sizzling sound.

A trail of smoke.

Cuddle Bunny Deluxe hopped off of me and ran away.

I turned to see Tommy holding the Super Soaker.

"Tommy!" I said. At that moment, I could honestly say that I'd never been so happy to see anyone in my life.

Tommy turned toward Sidekick Bunny and opened fire. A steady stream of holy water sprayed out and soaked him. Sidekick Bunny tried to hop away, but Tommy kept the Super Soaker locked on him.

Sidekick Bunny's fur sizzled and hissed. All over his body, little bubbles formed, looking like they would boil over. He howled and fell to the ground, writhing. Tommy kept it up until Sidekick Bunny melted like candle wax. All that was left behind was a puddle of furry goo.

Tommy looked over at me. "Are you okay?"

"Tommy, that was amazing! You saved my life!"

He smiled. "C'mon, you knew I wasn't going to let you do this alone."

I shook my head. "No, I really didn't. I thought you abandoned me, but you came through and that's all that counts." I looked over at the puddle of Bunny again. "You used a lot of water on him."

"What do you mean?"

"Nothing, I'm just saying that you used an awful lot of water on just one. I don't know what we're going to do. There are so many of them and I'm not sure we have enough water to get them all." I pushed the Hugging Hippo boxes to the side and got to my feet, accidentally kicking one as I did. The song went off.

"I hate that song," Tommy said.

"Yeah, so did the Cuddle Bunnies. I mean, like despised it. It drove them crazy." I told Tommy about their reaction.

He snapped his fingers. "Wait a second. Maybe that's it!"

"What?"

"That song! Your iPod!"

"What are you talking about?" I asked.

He stuck out his hand. "Give me your iPod!"

"Why?"

"Just give it to me!" he repeated.

I fished the iPod out of my pocket and handed it to him. "What are you thinking?"

Tommy tapped away at the screen until he came to the songs. "You remember before when the Cuddle Bunny song went off in the yard?"

"Yeah, so?"

He held the screen up to my face. "Look what's already downloaded on here."

I took the iPod from him and saw *The FAB Album: All your favorite songs from all your favorite toys!* "Why would my parents download this for me?"

"Never mind that," Tommy said. "Read the list. Third one down."

I scrolled down until I came to it. "The Hugging Hippo song."

Tommy nodded. "There's your answer. We play the song to keep them all away until we get to Mr. Flopsy-Ears."

"And then what?"

He reached into his pocket and removed the vial of reverse potion. "I was thinking about it while you were gone. All we have to do is use this on Mr. Flopsy-Ears. You know how with vampires, if you kill the main one, all the rest that he's turned into vampires become normal again?"

"But vampires aren't real," I said.

Tommy rolled his eyes. "I know, and neither are warlocks or living, evil stuffed animals. I bet it's the same thing with Cuddle Bunnies as with vampires. We use it on Mr. Flopsy-Ears and all the other Bunnies turn back. It's that simple."

"But there are probably like over a hundred of them out there right now."

He tapped the iPod in my hand. "The song. You use it to keep the others away and I'll hold them off with this." He held up the Super Soaker.

"I don't know. We're going on a hunch? What if you're wrong? Then we'll be right in the middle of a ton of those psycho little rabbits with nothing to protect us."

Tommy placed his hand on my shoulder. "Devin, trust me." He nodded. "We got this."

I studied his face. He looked very sure of himself. I thought back to all of the things he had tried before, which had been wrong, but yet he was still right about Herb being a warlock. And he did just save my life. Above all else, he had a plan and I didn't. As much as I hated to admit it, he was right. I needed to start trusting him. I sighed and shoved the iPod back into my pocket. "Okay."

Tommy smiled. "Don't worry. I know what I'm doing."

Behind Tommy, a streak of white rushed toward us.

I pointed. "Tommy, look out!"

Tommy whirled, but too late.

Cuddle Bunny Deluxe swung a bat right into Tommy's leg. A sickening, crunching sound could be heard, even over the Christmas music.

"Aaaaaaaah!" Tommy screamed and crumpled to the ground.

Cuddle Bunny Deluxe stood over him and raised the bat above his head.

Without thinking, I launched myself at the overgrown rabbit and knocked the bat out of his paws. We tumbled over and over until we rolled to a stop and started pounding on each other.

He pummeled me, while at the same time using his ears like flippers to smack me across the face.

I flailed away at him, but my shots seemed to have little effect. I realized pretty fast that this was not a fight I was going to win by regular means.

Cuddle Bunny Deluxe swiveled around in a blur. For such a big rabbit, he sure moved fast. He fastened his arm around my throat and squeezed, cutting off my air.

I couldn't breathe. The sounds of my wheezing grew louder.

Cuddle Bunny Deluxe tightened his grip. I clawed at his paw, but I'm not sure that he even felt it. If this kept up much longer, I wouldn't have a much longer. I reared back and elbowed him in the stomach, but it sank into his fluff-filled body. I started to get dizzy. I reached for his side and dragged my hand down until I found what I was searching for. His tag. Every stuffed animal had one. I grabbed it tightly and yanked.

He snarled in my ear, then punched the side of my face.

I used my other hand to block as best as I could, but didn't let go of the tag. I yanked again and felt it give a little.

A yelp of pain.

I looked back. Cuddle Bunny Deluxe's eyes widened. His expression changed. He didn't look as mean as before. Now, he looked worried. Scared.

I pulled again as hard as I could. This time I heard it. A tear along the seam.

He chomped down on my arm.

"Ow!" I screamed just as I found the tear in his side and thrust my arm in and grabbed a fistful of stuffing and wrenched it out.

Cuddle Bunny Deluxe howled in pain. He released his hold on me and tried to shove me away, but I held tight.

I reached in and yanked out more.

He fell to the floor and began pounding and kicking at it. He reminded me of Abby when she had one of her tantrums.

I jumped on him and didn't let up. Pulling stuffing out in a blur.

He turned quickly, grabbed my throat again, and squeezed tightly. His features were hard, savage. He wasn't going to let go. He wanted to kill me.

Dizziness set in. Little spots formed in front of my eyes. My vision blurred. If I didn't beat him now, I'd be dead and who knew what the Cuddle Bunnies would wind up doing. It was up to me. I was the only one who could stop them. Only me. My fingers closed in on the white fluffy, cottony stuffing that filled the Cuddle Bunny. I wrenched out fistful after fistful.

His forehead pressed against mine. His face inches away. His eyes fluttered. His hold on my throat grew weaker and weaker until finally it stopped. Cuddle Bunny Deluxe twitched a couple of times and then was still.

I pulled his paws from my throat, took a deep breath, and staggered over to Tommy. "Are you okay?"

A layer of sweat coated his forehead. "I think my leg is broken."

"I have to get you out of here," I said.

He shook his head. "There's no time now. I'll be okay, just get Mr. Flopsy-Ears." He handed me the Super Soaker. "Here, take this."

"What about you? What are you going to do if they come back?"

"I'm going to drag myself to the back and hide." He pointed over to the vial of reverse potion on the ground.

"Use it on Mr. Flopsy-Ears. All the others will turn back. I promise. I know this stuff."

I picked up the vial and stared at the blue liquid. "Okay, Tommy. I'll do it."

He looked pale. "You can do this, Devin."

I nodded. I wished I had as much faith in me as he did. "How will I find Mr. Flopsy-Ears, though? He could be anywhere."

"I thought about that too. Try to get them all to one place. But you'll need bait. Something they'll respond to. And that's obvious."

"Not so obvious, if I don't know it."

He pointed to me. "You're the bait. You and that Hugging Hippos song. They hate the Hugging Hippos so much, they'll do anything to stop it. Play that song. Wait for the Cuddle Bunnies. Drop reverse potion on Mr. Flopsy-Ears, and presto—" He snapped his fingers. "Cuddle Bunny threat is eliminated. It's easy."

I raised my hand. "Uh, I'm sorry, but you lost me right after the part where you said I was bait."

"Someone has to do it, Devin. I would, but you know, I broke my leg saving your life."

"Yeah, yeah. I'm never going to hear the end of that one, am I?"

He smiled. "Probably not. Now, go get Mr. Flopsy-Ears!"

"Okay." I took a step to go, but stopped and turned back to him. "And Tommy?"

"Yeah?"

"Thank you. You're a great friend."

Tommy frowned. "Seriously? Are you going to get all weepy and sentimental now?"

"No, I just—"

"I'm lying here with my leg broken, and you want to get all emotional? Go kill Mr. Flopsy-Ears already!"

"Okay, okay!"

I started walking toward the front of the store all alone, armed with a little less than half a container of holy water and a couple of drops of reverse potion, heading off to face an army of evil rabbits, and the only thing I could think of was that Mr. Flopsy-Ears had to pay.

CHAPTER NINETEEN

THE CALL OF THE HIPPOS

The mall outside the toy store was deserted now, but signs that the Cuddle Bunnies had been there were all over the place. Store windows were smashed in. Garbage and shopping bags were littered all over the ground. Kiosks overturned. It looked like an earthquake had hit.

All the stores were open and nobody was watching them. Nearby, the electronic store was abandoned. I probably could have taken anything I wanted and nobody would know about it. Normally, that would've been one of the coolest things ever, but not tonight. I thought about all the iPhones just lying around, but knew I couldn't do it. Funny how it didn't even seem that important to me now. Instead, all I could think about was how each overturned kiosk could be a Bunny hiding place. Each empty store a potential point of attack.

I aimed the Super Soaker all around, ready to fire at anything that moved. I had absolutely no idea where I was going or what I was going to do when I got there, but kept walking anyway. With each step, it hit me more and more that I was actually relying on Tommy's plan . . . and had no idea if it would even work. He was convinced that all I had to do was find Mr. Flopsy-Ears and get rid of him and all the rest of the Cuddle Bunnies would change back. Still, all the times Tommy had been wrong about something went through my mind. I hoped that this time he'd be right.

A voice blared out over the mall PA system, *"Attention shoppers, please remain calm. We are fully aware of the electrical problem which has short-circuited and locked the mall exits. Rest assured, we are presently working on the issue and hope to have everything back to being fully operational very shortly. As far as the reports about stuffed animals running loose, please do not be alarmed. We believe this to be nothing more than a promotional stunt by the FAB toy company. But just to be on the safe side, we advise you to make your way over to where mall security has been stationed, right by—hey, what are you doing in here? No! Get away from—"*

Static erupted over the speakers, lasting for several moments, before being replaced by "Christmas (Baby Please Come Home)."

That was it. The Cuddle Bunnies were growing more daring and dangerous. I had to get rid of them fast. Near me was an overturned perfume kiosk. It reminded me a little of the forts Tommy and I used to make when we were kids. Maybe I could use it as a barricade? I climbed behind it, crouched down, and pulled the iPod out of my pocket and scrolled through the songs until I came to it.

The Hugging Hippo Song.

Amazing. I still had no idea why Mom and Dad downloaded it for me or even thought I'd want it, but I guess now I had to be at least a little thankful that they were so out of touch. I puffed out a breath of air and pressed PLAY. I held the iPod above my head and peered out, scanning the surrounding area. I realized it could barely be heard over the Christmas music booming through the mall's PA system. This wasn't going to do anything. I needed to find a better way.

I was about to stand up from behind the kiosk when a white-furred blur leaped at me and knocked the iPod out of my hand, sending it flying several feet until it hit the floor and skidded to a stop.

I turned to see a Cuddle Bunny standing a few feet away. He was hunched over like a tiger ready to pounce. His fur stood on end. He eyed the iPod that now lay between us. His whiskers twitched.

He was going to destroy it.

Not today, Cuddle Bunny. I needed it.

I raised the Super Soaker, but he was faster. But instead of going for the iPod, he lunged at me. I hadn't expected that and fired wildly past him. He rammed me back against the side of the kiosk. The Super Soaker dropped from my hand. Bottles of perfume came crashing down around me, breaking and splattering all over.

My clothes were soaked with the smell. *Uch,* who likes this stuff?

The Cuddle Bunny grabbed my hair, jumped back, and stomped my face with both feet. He turned toward the iPod.

I couldn't let him have it.

He put his feet against my chest and pushed off, but not before I snatched his tail and yanked him back. "No, you don't!" I screamed and threw him against a nearby garbage can.

He tumbled over but rolled to his feet fast. His eyes blazed with hatred. In an instant, he charged.

I reached out for the Super Soaker, but instead my fingers grazed a small glass bottle. I grabbed it and brought it up just in time to spray a stream of perfume in the Cuddle Bunny's eyes.

It shrieked and dropped to the ground like a bird shot out of the sky.

Before it could get back to its feet, I threw the bottle and nailed it on the side of the head. It bounced off with a clunking sound. I scrambled for the Super Soaker and in one motion, grabbed it and swiveled toward the stuffed rabbit and fired the holy water, striking its shoulder.

Sizzle and smoke followed by a Bunny shriek. The Cuddle Bunny turned and hightailed it away.

"That's right, you better run!" I yelled after it, really hoping he wouldn't turn around and come back.

I rushed over to the iPod and examined it. Still intact. Those protective cases really worked. I checked the Super Soaker. Less than half a tank left. This wasn't going to cut it. Not if I kept wasting water on these underling Bunnies. I needed to get Mr. Flopsy-Ears.

A quick search of the area showed no trace of any other Cuddle Bunnies. The iPod had played as loud as it could go and only drew one. That wouldn't do. If I wanted to get them to me, I needed them to hear it. There was only one place I could think of where it was open enough for that to happen. The food court.

I ran, trying not to pay attention to anything but getting to where I needed to go.

All around me was destruction, but I raced on until to the side of me I heard, "Hey, kid! What are you doing? Hide!"

I turned as I ran and realized that the stores weren't empty at all. There were people in them. They were hiding behind the displays. Some of them waving me over.

Store after store, the same thing.

I ignored all of them. There was no time now.

Nothing stopped me until—"Devin!"

I skidded to a halt.

"Mom?"

To the right, hiding in a clothing store. My family.

"Devin, what are you doing here?" Mom said. "You went to the mall by yourself?"

I shook my head. "No, I came with Tommy."

"Did you bring Mr. Flopsy-Ears?" Abby asked.

"With Tommy?" Dad said. "Oh, that makes it perfectly okay."

"Are you out of your mind?" Mom said. "Get over here right now!"

"I'm sorry, I can't. I'm the only one who can fix this. I'll explain later." I took off.

"Devin!" she said.

She sounded angry, but I couldn't stop. Not now. I'd deal with her punishment later, but for now she'd have to wait because this couldn't. I raced on until finally, I reached it.

The food court.

I took a moment to catch my breath as I took everything in. Right outside of the food court was an enormous Christmas tree. It must have been at least twenty feet high. Directly in front of it was a large red chair for taking pictures with Santa. He was long gone by now, but a Cuddle Bunny in a Santa cap and white beard was sitting in his place. Another Cuddle Bunny sat on his lap reading a list off of a long sheet of paper. Behind them were several more waiting in line to take their turns.

In the middle of the food court was a large circular fountain. A few Cuddle Bunnies frolicked in it, using their ears like paddles to splash each other with water.

They seemed very caught up in what they were doing, which allowed me to sneak past and hide behind some tables.

It looked like a disaster area. Food trays had been left everywhere. Cuddle Bunnies were gorging themselves on the remains. Overturned drink cups made mini-waterfalls spilling off the edge of the tables. To the right, some Cuddle Bunnies were in the Burger King. One was lying under the Coke slushie machine with its mouth open while another held the nozzle and aimed a steady stream of frozen drink into it. The Bunny's stomach swelled with slushie until he rolled off and fell to the counter below. Another Cuddle Bunny jumped on his bloated belly, sending a spray of projectile slushie fountaining up over both of them, streaking them with little brown spots. They both erupted in laughter.

To the left, by the Italian food place, two Cuddle Bunnies were eating spaghetti from a heating tin. They didn't realize they were slurping up two ends of the same strand until their lips smacked together. One of them laughed until the other grabbed a pan and clunked him on the head, knocking the laughing Bunny to the ground, before continuing to devour the spaghetti.

I scanned the storefronts until I found one with no Bunnies in it. A health-food store. These must have been the only bunnies in the world who didn't like vegetables. I crept over as quietly as I could, hopped over the counter, and dropped behind it, taking a deep breath to calm myself. I'd made it, but I wasn't done. Not by a long shot.

Here came the fun part. I placed the Super Soaker on the counter and searched for the microphone and found it near the register. *Here goes nothing.*

I flipped the microphone button on and placed the iPod on the counter next to it. A loud whistling pierced the air. The Cuddle Bunnies in the food court all stopped what they were doing and whipped their heads in my direction.

A sea of black, beady Bunny eyes met mine. They all narrowed simultaneously.

Uh-oh.

Like an angry hive of bees, they swarmed toward me.

"This better work," I muttered and hit play on the iPod.

I'm a Hugging Hippo blared out, halting the mass of Cuddle Bunnies dead in their tracks, all of them covering their ears at once. Their faces twisted in agony.

They hated that song.

I'm your Hugging friend

Howls of Bunny torment filled the air, followed by snarls and hisses.

I stared out over the counter and was surprised at how fast the Bunny mob had multiplied. What I thought had been only a few Cuddle Bunnies in the food court was now a horde of well over a hundred and growing. They had probably all been around this area and I hadn't even seen them. That scared me even more. They could be anywhere.

I scanned the faces and compared the slight differences on each one, realizing how ironic it was that just as I was about to die, I was becoming a Cuddle Bunny expert. Still, with as many differences as each Bunny had, they did have one thing in common. They all looked like they wanted to kill me.

Actually, there was also one other thing they all had in common. None of them got within five feet of the counter. It was like the amplified Hugging Hippo song provided an invisible barrier around me.

I swerved the Super Soaker back and forth to keep them away while praying they didn't realize how stacked the odds were in their favor. If they all charged at once, I'd be finished.

After several moments, I finally spotted what I'd been searching for. Three rows deep into the mass of Bunnies, a bent ear.

Mr. Flopsy-Ears.

I reached into my pocket and felt the vial of reverse potion. I'd have to do this fast. I went over my plan. First, I would spray the front rows of Bunnies with the holy water. Second, before they knew what was happening, I'd jump out and knock the wounded Bunnies out of the way. Third, I'd grab Mr. Flopsy-Ears and use the reverse potion on him, turning him back into a lifeless stuffed animal. Fourth, they'd all turn back right after him. Fifth, I'd go back and save Tommy. And last, I'd be a hero and Mom would have no choice but to not punish me and to buy me an iPhone.

It wouldn't be easy, but maybe, just maybe, it could work.

I closed my eyes for a second and took a deep breath. *Please let this work.* I opened them, looked out into the crowd, and prepared myself to jump.

That's when my iPod died.

CHAPTER TWENTY

SHOWDOWN AT THE FOOD COURT

Twenty-seven seconds.

That's how long it took the Cuddle Bunnies to realize the iPod had died before they attacked. First they inched their paws away from their ears. Next, they looked at each other, like they were checking to make sure the Hugging Hippo song was really gone. And then . . . the stampede.

A bunch of bouncing Bunnies bounded for me.

I swung the Super Soaker from side to side and fired wildly, hoping to strike anything. I hit some and heard the sizzling sound, but there were just too many of them. In almost no time, they swarmed over me.

The Super Soaker was ripped from my hands as the Bunnies clustered on top of me. I lashed out with everything I had, but my punches didn't seem to have much effect. Wave after wave of Cuddle Bunnies struck.

White fur was everywhere. I grabbed and pulled at tags, hoping to tear the seams. I managed to rip some open and grab their stuffing, but their numbers were too great. They just kept coming and coming and coming, their beady black button eyes filled with murder and mayhem.

They piled on top of me, burying me under a heap of furry little bodies. I couldn't breathe.

Bunny paws pummeled and pounded me. Bunny teeth chewed and chomped.

I started to panic. I couldn't believe I was going to die at the hands—paws—of some crazy, come-to-life stuffed animals.

"I hate you!" I said. "I hate every single one of you!"

I wrenched stuffing from any Cuddle Bunny I could get my hands on, but there were just too many. If something didn't happen fast, there was no doubt they would finish me off.

I started to think of Mom and Dad and even Abby, when suddenly, all at once, the Cuddle Bunnies stopped, released their hold, and sprang up. Like a herd of gazelle detecting a predator, their heads turned at once. All of their ears perked up and twitched in unison.

I listened, but couldn't hear anything except for the Christmas music. No, wait . . . there was something more. Something faint, but familiar . . . and it was getting closer.

The Cuddle Bunnies glanced at each other. Their fur ruffled. None of them were concentrating on me anymore.

The Super Soaker was lying on the floor only a few feet away. I scrambled for it before pulling myself up to the counter to be able to hear the sound better. It was music. I knew it from somewhere, but what was it?

The song grew louder. The lyrics became clearer.

It hit me. My eyes widened. *The Hugging Hippo song*!

I looked down the counter where I'd left the iPod and ran to get it, wondering if it had started playing again, but the screen was dark. The battery was still dead.

I turned back toward the sound and finally saw where it was coming from. There, past the courtyard, on the other side of the fountain by the huge Christmas tree, headed this way . . . a pod of gray-furred Hugging Hippos! They stood on two feet, marching like soldiers, singing that stupid song as they went.

I'm a Hugging Hippo
I'm your Hugging friend
We'll always be together
I'll follow you to the end

"What the—" I said.

A nearby Cuddle Bunny and I glanced at each other and shrugged.

I blasted him with a shot of holy water.

He shrieked and scampered away.

The Cuddle Bunnies let out a collective hiss. They all acted like they had completely forgotten I was there. They jumped onto the counter and growled at the approaching Hippos.

A whistling pierced the air.

The Cuddle Bunnies froze.

I turned along with them toward the sound.

In the center of the food court, standing on a table, was Mr. Flopsy-Ears. He lifted his paw above his head, looked over the assembly of Cuddle Bunnies, and nodded.

Together, the other Bunnies nodded back.

Mr. Flopsy-Ears swiped his paw down.

The Cuddle Bunnies let out an angry howl, like a war-cry. They sang their own song in response.

I'm your furry bestie

Never need to test me

Because one thing will always be true

No matter where you go, I will find you

The Bunnies rushed the now-charging Hugging Hippos.

The warring armies collided in the center of the food court. Hippos squeezing Bunnies. Bunnies kicking Hippos. Fur and stuffing flying everywhere.

I crouched behind the counter, watching the savage display in front of me. For the moment, they all seemed too busy destroying each other to think about me, but I knew that wouldn't last.

I also realized I had another problem as well. No matter which side won, I would lose.

I had no idea if the Hugging Hippos liked people or not, but I couldn't wait to find out. If they didn't, I'd be in the same exact situation, only with Hippos instead of Bunnies. I checked the Super Soaker. Not much holy water left. There was no way I'd be able to get all of them.

Tommy's words came back to me. According to him, I wouldn't need to. I'd only need to get one: Mr. Flopsy-Ears. He said if I took care of Mr. Flopsy-Ears all the rest would turn back to normal. I had no idea if that would work on the Hippos also or if there was even a Hippo leader to focus on, but it didn't matter. Mr. Flopsy-Ears was my target. I had to take him out and hope for the best.

Already, signs of the carnage were starting to pile up everywhere, with Hippo and Bunny parts scattered all around.

How was I going to find Mr. Flopsy-Ears through all of this?

I scanned the battle. All around me was fighting. Right in front, a Hippo was swinging a Bunny by the ears above his head before launching him through the air. Two other Bunnies then jumped on the Hippo's back and chomped down on his shoulders.

Thankfully, they were inflicting all this damage on each other and not on me. I looked past them and kept searching until I spotted him by the fountain. Mr. Flopsy-Ears was holding a Hippo's head under the water. This was my chance. I patted my pocket to make sure the vial of reverse potion was still there and gripped the Super Soaker tight. It was now or never. I took a deep breath and vaulted over the counter.

Like a bull, I charged through the fighting, kicking Bunnies and Hippos out of the way as I went. I imagined I was in the middle of some old war movie, storming a beach, with bodies falling all around me.

As I neared Mr. Flopsy-Ears, some of the other Cuddle Bunnies seemed to sense what I was doing and left their Hugging Hippo foes to rush me instead. I mowed a couple of them down with the Super Soaker, never stopping or slowing down.

Only a few yards more. I couldn't believe it, but I was going to make it. Straight ahead, with his back turned to me, still holding the Hugging Hippo under the fountain water, was Mr. Flopsy-Ears. Maybe I could ambush him without him ever knowing. Please let it be that easy.

I raised the Super Soaker and took aim.

Bye-bye, Mr. Flopsy-Ears.

Before I could pull the trigger, out of the corner of my eye, a streak of white hurtled toward me. I turned, but it was too late. It rammed into my arm, sending the Super Soaker flying away into the fighting mob.

"Nooooooo!"

Mr. Flopsy-ears turned away from the fountain and faced me. For that instant, it felt like all the other Bunnies and Hippos disappeared from the food court. It was only me and Mr. Flopsy-Ears staring each other down, like two gunslingers in an old western movie. I could almost hear the whistling theme music in the background.

His face wrinkled. He balled his paws into little fists. His whiskers twitched.

I wriggled my fingers. I needed to be nimble now. I reached into my pocket to fish out the reverse potion, shielding it in my palm.

The two of us faced each other, without moving, sizing the other up. He was mine, and he had to go down. I gritted my teeth, let out a yell, and charged.

Mr. Flopsy-Ears' eyes widened. He didn't look like he'd been expecting that.

I rocketed into him, sending us both crashing into the fountain. That horrible feeling of being in wet clothing overwhelmed me, breaking my concentration for a moment. That was all it took. I saw Mr. Flopsy-Ears' fist right before it struck my face.

I toppled back helplessly as he pounced on me, grabbed my hair, and shoved my head under the water.

I thrashed about, still trying to hold onto the vial. If I lost that, it was over.

Next to me was another face. Two dull eyes staring back into mine.

It startled me until I realized it was the lifeless carcass of the Hugging Hippo that Mr. Flopsy-Ears had drowned. If I didn't want to meet the same fate, I needed to act fast. I thrust my hand up, grabbed Mr. Flopsy-Ears' whiskers, and yanked him down under the water with me. It was enough of a shock to get him to release his hold.

I pushed him off and raised my head above water, gasping for air.

Mr. Flopsy-Ears got up too. His fur was soaked. His long bunny ears hung down to the sides, drooping and dripping. His lip curled up and he snarled.

I grabbed the top of the cork stopper in the vial and pulled—it wouldn't budge! It was stuck.

"Oh, come on!" I said. "You've got to be kidding me!"

Mr. Flopsy-Ears kicked up at my arms, knocking the vial out of my hands and into the other side of the fountain, where it floated around the centerpiece and out of sight.

I raced after it, but Mr. Flopsy-Ears was on me fast.

He jumped on my shoulders and hammered his fists into the sides of my head before shoving me under water again.

I alligator-rolled in the fountain. Spinning over and over, trying to make it difficult for him to hold on.

His hold on me loosened and I sprang to my feet and looked down at the wet rabbit.

He glared at me.

"I hate you, Mr. Flopsy-Ears!" I shouted and kicked him hard, right in his stomach, punting him into the air. I ran to get the vial and found it still intact.

Mr. Flopsy-Ears landed about thirty yards away. He shook his body like a wet dog and sent little water pellets flying off his fur. His eyes found mine. He bared his bunny teeth and grabbed another Cuddle Bunny, who had just wasted a Hungry Hippo, and pointed at me.

The other Bunny looked over and nodded.

Together, they charged.

"Come on!" I said and tugged at the cork stopper again.

Twenty-five yards away.

I felt a little give to it and kept pulling.

Twenty.

"Please . . ."

Fifteen.

I winced and in one last-ditch effort, popped the cork stopper free of the vial.

"Yes!" I screamed as the force from the released pressure sent my arms flying back, where I heard the unmistakable sound of breaking glass.

My heart sank. I glanced back, but already knew. My hand had struck the centerpiece of the fountain. The bottom of the vial was gone, with jagged edges running along where the glass had smashed. The last of the potion was dripping down into the fountain.

I looked down at the water to see a small blue puddle floating on the surface. It only lasted a second or two, before dissolving into the water.

"Nooooo!" I stared at the water, forgetting for the moment about the attacking Bunnies.

Luckily, I noticed two white streaks at the last second and ducked the first one as I saw Mr. Flopsy-Ears sail over me. Unfortunately, I couldn't dodge the second, sending the two of us sprawling back into the water.

He was on me fast and shoved me back under.

Every part of my body screamed in agony. The fight with Mr. Flopsy-Ears had taken a toll and I had no idea where I would get the strength to fight this one, but I knew giving up would mean death.

I swung, kicked, and lashed out, but he was too strong. Through the water, I could make out his grinning Bunny face.

He was enjoying this. This was it. He was going to kill me. Sadness washed over me. If I wasn't already under the water, I knew for sure I would've felt the tears on my cheeks.

I looked up into his jeering eyes, when suddenly something strange happened. The smile disappeared from my Cuddle Bunny strangler. His eyes went wide and his head flopped to the side. He released his hold and dropped.

I jumped up and gulped down several breaths of air. *What happened?* I staggered to my feet and stared down at the now-lifeless Cuddle Bunny in the water. Next to him floated the cork stopper from the vial of reverse potion.

It took me a moment to realize what had just happened. "No way," I whispered. The reverse potion in the water must have turned him back. There was no other explanation I could think of.

I looked up to see Mr. Flopsy-Ears several feet away.

His jaw dropped. He eyed the fountain, seemed to understand what had happened, and turned and scampered away.

"Get back here!" I yelled, knowing how stupid I sounded. No way was he coming back, but I couldn't let him get away. *What do I do?*

I searched the food court frantically, trying to come up with something. "Come on . . . think," I said. I watched the fighting FABs and scanned the stores in the food court. The garbage on the floor. The spigots on the ceiling. "Wait . . ."

"The mall is going green." Dad had said that many times. The mall was recycling its water. He made a big deal about it in his boring stories. Maybe . . . ?

I scooped up some water in my hands and tossed it on a nearby Cuddle Bunny.

He froze like he had been turned to stone and dropped to the ground.

I looked down to the water in the fountain and then back to the spigots on the ceiling. Did the water in the fountain recycle through the mall also? I got an idea that might be my only hope.

I jumped out of the fountain and ran back toward the Italian food booth. The number of FABs had decreased a lot, while the amount of Bunny and Hippo parts had increased. They had done a number on each other, but there were still plenty left.

I bounded over the counter to get to the kitchen area. Open flames were still on the stove. I searched the nearby items, looking for something that could burn well. My eyes came to rest on a stack of paper plates.

Bingo!

I grabbed them and held one of them to the fire until it lit and eased my hand back, being careful not to let the flame go out.

With my paper-plate torch and another stack in hand, I eased myself back over the counter, which wasn't exactly easy to do while holding an open flame, and made my way toward the center of the food court.

Because of the fire, all the FAB toys seemed to notice me and stopped what they were doing. There was no more fighting as they all stared at the flame in my hand and turned toward me. This had caught their attention. A low growl erupted from the mob, but it wasn't directed at each other. Now, they all focused on me and closed in. Lucky me, I had managed to unite Hugging Hippo and Cuddle Bunny for a common goal . . . my death.

I waved the plate back and forth. "Get back!" They flinched every time the flame got near them. "I'm warning all of you, stay away!"

I reached a table in the center and placed the stack of plates down and lit them, keeping an eye on all the FABs. I circled the table slowly to keep them at bay, while grabbing napkins and other plates from the surrounding tables to add to my fire.

The growls and snarls surrounded me and grew louder. One moment of not paying attention and the FABs would pounce. I waited and waited, trying to hold off the mob, until finally the fire grew large enough to make an impact.

Smoke drifted up toward the ceiling.

Please let this work.

I circled and circled the table, waving the lit plate in front, when a black object struck my hand, knocking the plate out.

"OW!" I rubbed my hand.

On the floor was the napkin dispenser somebody had thrown.

The growls grew louder.

I looked out into the angry faces of the FAB mob. "Oh, cra—"

Bunny and Hippo united and jumped on top of me until I was buried under a pile of furry bodies.

"Get off of me!"

No matter which part of my body I covered up, it wasn't enough as they struck every unprotected area. Then, the biting. It was like I was out in the jungle being devoured by a pack of wild animals.

Just as they got too much for me, the sound that I had been waiting for saved me . . . the bell.

The clanging of the fire alarm.

The FABs let go of me and looked up toward the ringing. The overhead spigots opened and soon blue water showered down all over the food court.

Almost instantly, FAB after FAB dropped like lifeless sacks. One by one they toppled over until the food court was littered with little carcasses.

I closed my eyes for a minute and let the water hit me and did the first thing that I felt.

I laughed. After all that, after all that I'd been through, water was what saved me.

I staggered to my feet and looked out over the field of fallen FABs and punched the air. "Yes!" The water in the fountain had recirculated into the mall's water system, just like Dad said it would. Maybe I should listen to his boring stories a little more often. I climbed up on the table and reached for the sky. "I did it!" After a few minutes the water stopped and I smiled. I really did it.

"Devin!"

I winced. Mom's voice. I turned to see her, Dad, Abby, and Tommy standing right outside the food court. Tommy leaned on Dad's shoulder.

"Will you get down off of that table!" Mom said.

"Mom!" I yelled and hopped down and ran through the FAB battleground until I reached her, throwing my arms around her waist for a big hug.

She lifted my chin to meet her face. "Are you okay, Devin?"

"Yeah, Mom. Listen, I know you're angry about me coming to the mall, but—"

She held up her hand to cut me off. "Tommy already explained everything."

"He did?" I asked.

Dad nodded. "Yeah." He looked away for a second before turning back to me. "Devin, I'm sorry we didn't believe you before. If you said something, I should've known that you weren't making it up. I have nothing else to say, but I apologize, and I promise that it won't happen again. From now on, I'm there for you, no matter what. I hope you forgive me."

I smiled up at him. "Yeah, Dad." I looked over at Tommy. His face looked green. "Tommy, are you all right?"

"Yeah," he said weakly. "But my leg is definitely broken."

"We better get you to a doctor," Dad said.

"Tommy," I said. "The Hippos . . . did you?"

He nodded. "Yeah. When you left, I started crawling to the back to hide, when I found the red potion. I realized that it was the same thing that Cuddle Bunny Deluxe was using to bring the others to life. I figured the Hugging Hippos and Cuddle Bunnies hated each other and thought maybe activating the Hippos would help you."

I hugged him. "It did. You saved my life!"

He smiled. "Twice! Don't forget that part. It was twice. Now, will someone please get me to the hospital? Everybody seems to be forgetting that my leg is broken!"

"Mr. Flopsy-Ears!" Abby shrieked.

Everyone turned toward her.

My heart thumped. "What? Where?"

She pointed all over the food court. "He isn't here! I looked everywhere. Where's Mr. Flopsy-Ears?"

"No . . ." I said. "Don't tell me." I ran all over the food court, from FAB to FAB, until I examined every single one. Abby was right. Mr. Flopsy-Ears wasn't here. "How can that be?" I muttered.

"What's wrong?" Dad asked.

"She's right," I said. "He's not here."

Dad shrugged. "So, what's the big deal? One Cuddle Bunny can't do much damage. We'll call the police. They'll take care of it."

"No. By the time they investigate and ask questions, it'll be too late. Dad, we have to stop him!"

"Us?" Dad said. "What are you talking about?"

I looked up at him. "Dad, please. If you meant what you said before about believing me always, I need you right now. I'll explain everything on the way, but I need you."

Dad stared back at me for a few moments. His features softened. He nodded. "Okay, Devin. What do you want me to do?"

"We need to go after him. Fast."

"But we have no idea where he is. He could be anywhere by now."

I shook my head. "No, Dad. I know exactly where he went."

CHAPTER TWENTY-ONE

FABCorp

As Dad drove me to the FAB factory, many thoughts went through my mind. The main one was, just how was I going to stop Mr. Flopsy-Ears? I had no holy water, no reverse potion, no anything. Not even Tommy, who I really could've used right around now. He was on his way to the emergency room with Mom and Abby, which meant this was all going to be up to me. At least Dad was with me this time. It felt good for him to be with me, instead of having to convince him of anything.

He slowed down as we pulled into the FAB parking lot. It was mostly dark, with only a few patches of light from some widely spaced street lamps. Several snow mounds had been piled high to clear the area for cars to park. Dad pulled in behind one of them, so he could be in the shadows. Other than one car parked close to the entrance, the lot was completely empty.

"Nobody should be able to see us here," Dad said.

"Yeah," I agreed, not really paying attention to the words, but instead staring out the windows, looking for any sign of Mr. Flopsy-Ears. With the snow on the ground and it being mostly dark, he could be standing right in front of me and I'd still have a very difficult time seeing him.

Dad peered through the windshield. "Are you sure he's coming here? It's kind of dark."

I scanned the area. "Yeah, Mr. Flopsy-Ears wants to bring all the other Cuddle Bunnies to life. This is the place." I pointed to the factory. "They're all inside."

Dad looked out again. "But the place is locked, Dev. I don't think there's any way for him to get inside even."

"He's a Bunny, Dad. He can get in."

"All right," Dad said. "Let's go take a look. But keep quiet. I have no idea what I'd even tell anybody if they asked why we were here."

"Tell them we were trying to get a FAB for Christmas and all the stores were sold out."

Dad remained quiet for a moment before speaking. I could practically see the wheels spinning inside his head. "Do you think that'd work? Maybe they'd give us one for free, since we made a special trip?"

"Dad, they're evil! We're not getting one!"

He thought a second. "Well, I'm only saying it because Abby lost hers and—"

"Dad!"

He held up his hands. "Okay, okay. No more Cuddle Bunnies."

"I should've taken Mom."

"No, no. I got this. Now, let's go hunt us some wabbits."

I rolled my eyes. "Seriously, Dad?"

He frowned. "Sorry. Let's go." He motioned for me to be quiet and opened the car door.

I crawled across the seat and out his side, so as not make any additional noise, and eased the door closed until I heard a click.

Dad pointed his car remote and pressed it. The car beeped and the lights flashed.

I winced. "Dad!"

"Sorry," he whispered. "But I only have seven payments left and I'm not going to let anything happen to it now." He motioned with his head. "Let's go."

We trudged toward the factory through the snow, which wasn't easy since it was deep and each step made a crunching sound as I sank in up to my calf.

If that noise didn't alert everybody we were coming, then I was sure my pounding heart would. To my ears, it sounded like a drum solo in a concert.

I kept my eyes peeled and searched all around us until I noticed something on the ground. "Dad, look!"

"What?"

I pointed down to the snow. "Bunny tracks. They're leading to the factory. C'mon!" I picked up the pace and followed the tracks as best as I could until we reached the front gates, which were locked. To the side of us was another massive snow mound, which they had cleared away from the entrance. The tracks reached the gate, but then disappeared. "Where'd he go?" I looked all around and then grabbed the bars of the gate to look through, but didn't see anything. "Dad, the tracks stop around here. He can't be far!"

Dad grabbed the bars too and pressed his face between them. "I don't see any more."

"Freeze!" someone shouted.

Dad sighed. "Great."

We turned toward the voice.

A security guard was standing next to the parked car by the entrance. He held a flashlight in one hand and a gun in the other. "Get your hands up where I can see them!"

Dad and I raised our arms above our heads.

"Let me do the talking," Dad whispered. "And don't say anything about magical Cuddle Bunnies either."

The guard came slowly toward us. I saw nothing but a shadow until he crossed into a ray of light and came into view. He was a short, chubby man whose coat was stretched open and looked like it was a good two sizes too small for him, almost forcing him to keep his arms stiffly out in front, like they were tied to two planks of wood. The buttons of his shirt looked like they were fighting a losing battle to keep it closed. This guy must have been who they modeled the Hugging Hippo after. The worst thing of all? Even though it was night, he wore dark sunglasses. Just my luck, we had to get stopped by some cop wannabe.

He waved the flashlight beam back and forth over us. "Well, well, well . . . looks like we got ourselves a couple of thieves."

Dad held his hands out in front of him. "Sir, this is a huge mistake, and I apologize. It's not what it looks like. I mean, do we look like thieves to you?"

The guard shrugged. "I don't like to profile anyone. In my eyes, anybody's perfectly capable of being a thief. Now, get your hands back up!" He flicked his gun hand up several times.

"That's not what I meant," Dad said. "I just—"

"Hands!" the guard yelled.

"Okay, okay!" Dad raised his arms again.

I couldn't take this anymore. I had to jump in. "We're not here to steal anything. We came out because we were hoping to get a Cuddle Bunny for Christmas and the stores are sold out."

The guard eyed me up and down. "You're a little old for a Cuddle Bunny, ain't ya?"

"It's not for me!" I said.

Dad swatted my head. "Quiet!" He turned back to the guard. "It's for my daughter. Sir, I don't know if you have kids or not . . ."

"Me?" He shook his head. "Nah, I'm not the settling down type. No one woman can hold me."

"Neither can those buttons," I said under my breath.

Dad swatted me again. "I understand. But I need a Cuddle Bunny for my little girl and don't want her to be disappointed if she doesn't get one. Do you understand what I'm saying?"

The guard looked at Dad for a couple of more seconds and then over at me again before finally lowering his arm. "Yeah, I guess I do." He holstered his gun.

I exhaled. "Dad, Mr. Flopsy-Ears. We have to—"

"I'm afraid the factory is closed for the holiday," the guard said.

Dad nodded. "Yeah, that's what I figured."

"Locked tighter than Fort Knox," the guard said. "The only way to get in there is with a key, which only the most trusted employees have." He smiled. "Like I happen to have right here." He patted his coat pocket.

"They must really love you," I said and turned back to Dad. This was taking forever, "Dad, Mr. Flopsy-Ears—"

Dad grabbed my shoulder. "Well, I'm sorry to take up your time. We'll be on our way." He turned to go.

I grabbed his arm. "Dad, we really need to get inside!"

The guard thrust his arm out and stopped Dad from walking. "The young fella is right. I'm a reasonable guy. Perhaps there's some sort of arrangement which could be made."

"Yeah?" Dad said. "What sort of arrangement?"

"I didn't say this wasn't open for discussion. But you do know on eBay they're going for a few hundred bucks, so it all depends on how bad do you want this toy?"

"A few hundred bucks?" Dad blurted.

The guard rubbed his chin and reached into his coat pocket, where he pulled out a large metallic ring with a ton of keys attached to it. He swirled the ring around his finger. "I guess it'd be a shame if your little girl didn't get a Cuddle Bunny for Christmas."

Dad glanced at me.

I nodded. "Dad, let him show us inside!"

"Not for a few hundred bucks," Dad said to me under his breath.

I barely caught what Dad said. My attention shifted to the snow mound behind him. Some snow started to shift and slide down.

I swatted his arm. "Dad!"

The guard continued. "You know, for that price, I'm sure I could probably make it happen."

More snow started falling, this time like a mini-landslide.

I pointed. "Dad!"

Dad turned to me. "What is it, Devin?"

Before I could answer, the mound exploded. Snow shot out in all directions. Mr. Flopsy-Ears burst through.

Everybody screamed. The beam of light swiveled in the air as the flashlight fell to the ground.

Before we knew what was happening, Mr. Flopsy-Ears grabbed Dad and the guard by their heads and rammed them together with a sickening clunking sound. They collapsed to the ground in a heap. Mr. Flopsy-Ears jumped out of the snow pile, grabbed the guard's handcuffs, clasped one end to the guard, looped the other end through the bars of the gate and back around, and clinched the other end to Dad. He then snatched the guard's key ring off the ground and squeezed through the bars of the gate. Once on the other side, he stopped and saluted me before hopping off toward the factory.

"No!" I said. "Dad, come on, get up! Mr. Flopsy-Ears is getting away."

Dad groaned and moved his hand toward his head, but it was snagged back by the handcuff. He fell back against the gate, blinked several times, and stared at me. "What happened?"

"Mr. Flopsy-Ears was here. He took the keys and he's getting away."

Dad tugged at the handcuff. "I'm stuck." He jostled the guard. "Hey, c'mon! Get up!"

The guard stirred. "Wha?"

"Get up!" Dad repeated. "You have to get the handcuffs off of us."

The guard sat up slowly and rubbed the side of his head with his other hand. "What's going on here?"

"We were attacked," Dad said. "And now we're hand-cuffed together."

The guard yanked at the handcuff. He looked around the area and patted the ground. "My keys. Where are my keys?"

"He took the keys!" I said.

"Oh, this is not good," the guard said. "The FAB Corporation isn't gonna like this."

"They don't have to know," Dad said. "Just unlock us and nobody will say a thing."

"I can't. My key is on that ring."

"Why do you keep your handcuff key on that ring?" Dad yelled.

"What are you, my boss?" He rubbed his head. "Am I imagining things or were we just attacked by a Cuddle Bunny? It must've hit me harder than I thought."

I looked at Dad. "Mr. Flopsy-Ears is probably inside by now. We have to go!"

Dad turned to the guard. "Can you shoot the cuffs off of us?"

The guard's head dropped. "The gun's not real," he said.

"What?" Dad said.

"They don't let us carry them. I could get in trouble if they even knew I had it. You won't say anything, will you?"

Dad gritted his teeth. "You are the worst security guard I've ever seen."

The guard frowned. "Hey, is that nice?"

"Devin," Dad said. "I'm sorry, but it's over. We tried, but it's no use. We're stuck."

I kept looking back and forth between Dad, the guard, and the snow on the other side of the gate. I needed to cross over and this was doing nothing to ease things.

"Dad, Mr. Flopsy-Ears is right on the other side of this fence! We have to get over."

"What do you want me to do, Devin? In case you didn't notice, I'm handcuffed to the gate."

I looked at the factory through the bars before turning to the pile of snow behind Dad and nodding. "You are . . . but I'm not."

Dad followed my eyes. "Devin, no! Do not even think about it. You are not going in there alone." He lunged for me, but I jumped out of his reach.

"I'm sorry, Dad." I grabbed the guard's flashlight.

"Devin, no!"

I ran to the other side of the snow pile. I worked my way to the top and realized it was still at least a foot away from the gate and appeared to be a nice drop on the other side. The wind picked up, causing me to sway a little bit. I steadied myself.

"Devin, do *not* do this!" Dad shouted. "If you get hurt, your mother will kill me. Do not try this!"

"I don't think we're insured for this," the guard said.

"Sorry, Dad." I took a deep breath. "I have to." Before I could change my mind, I leaped.

CHAPTER TWENTY-TWO

SHOWDOWN WITH MR. FLOPSY-EARS

I followed the snowy path to the factory door, which was already open a crack. Mr. Flopsy-Ears had to be inside. I nudged it open, trying not to make a sound, and peered into the darkness. The only thing I could see was shadows. This was not good, but I had no choice. I stepped in.

The first thing that hit me was the smell. Burnt fumes. Like gas or oil. The heat wasn't on, though, and it was cold in here. Not too much of a difference from outside.

There were machines all over the place. So many dark places to hide. Mr. Flopsy-Ears could be anywhere. I waved the flashlight back and forth in front of me. I needed to find the light switch and fast. The darkness was too much of an advantage for him.

I inched my way through, trying to keep a look out for anything, but it was so tough to see. The shadows played tricks on me. I could swear I saw movements in all directions.

I backed slowly toward the wall, reaching out behind me, searching for the switch, when I hit something. Something furry.

I whirled the flashlight around to come face to face with two black Cuddle Bunny eyes staring right back at me.

"Aaaaaaaagh!" I jumped away and banged into something.

The flashlight fell to the floor, where it spun around, shining its beam in a circle around me. Cuddle Bunny faces were everywhere. My heart raced out of control, the sound drumming in my head.

I scrambled for the flashlight, snatched it off the floor, and aimed it back at the Bunny faces. They were still there. They hadn't moved. I kept the beam fixed on them, then exhaled. They were just shells. Cuddle Bunny skins that hadn't been filled with stuffing yet, hanging from a metal rack.

Everything in me trembled. This was frazzling my nerves. I turned toward the wall and searched near the door until I saw a red button and rushed over and pressed it. A small electric sound crackled above me and the lights flickered on.

The first thing that hit me was just how enormous this place was, even bigger than I imagined. A combination of warehouse and factory, filled with machines and Bunnies. Above me, row after row of Cuddle Bunny shells hung from racks. There had to be at least a couple of hundred of them in a line, stretching all the way across the room. It was creepy to see their opened, flat bodies before their stuffing went in. They reminded me of bearskin rugs, where the body was flat and only the head was left intact.

A conveyor belt snaked its way around the room. Every so often above it there was some sort of station for putting the FAB together. From sewing to stuffing and then sewing again.

Cuddle Bunnies lay along the surface of the conveyor belt in various stages of assembly.

Suddenly, I heard a loud clicking sound followed by a metallic hum as the machines whirred to life. The conveyor belt started to roll. I turned toward the spot the clicking had come from and saw a control panel with a key inserted into it. Dangling from the key was a loop with other keys on it. The same key ring the guard had had outside and Mr. Flopsy-Ears had taken! Mr. Flopsy-Ears had been right there! But where was he now?

In spite of the cold, I felt a bead of sweat trickle down my forehead. My whole body tingled. I looked about in every direction as I followed the path of the conveyor belt, practically hugging the side for protection. Robotic arms came down and grabbed a Bunny shell before filling it with stuffing.

A little further along, a large metal needle, like an oversized sewing machine, started following a pattern and stitching the cloth together. Cuddle Bunnies were being created at a rapid pace and that wasn't good. No matter what, I couldn't allow them to be brought to life.

The overhead racks of Bunny skins began to swing toward the conveyor belt, edging past me on the way. A mechanized arm plucked one after another off the rack to place on the belt for stuffing. I pushed them out of the way so I could get a clear view of the factory, but there were so many of them. It wasn't good to be blinded even for a second, with Mr. Flopsy-Ears on the loose.

The racks of shells kept swinging by, sending furry Bunny-pelts brushing against my skin. I felt claustrophobic and shoved each of them away from my face as they passed. All I could see was white fur as they engulfed me. The machine sped up and the line of Bunnies blurred.

As I watched each pelt swing by, my legs trembled. I expected each one to attack me. That's when I saw it. One of them blinked. Before I could move, one of the skins reached down and gripped my wrist.

Mr. Flopsy-Ears!

He grinned.

My heart stopped. My mouth was dry. My hands were shaking.

He swung back, but then came forward fast, landing his big Bunny feet flush into my face.

I staggered. My knees buckled and my head spun. I saw stars, but couldn't black out now. If I did, I was done for.

I lunged for him, but he was too fast and hopped out of my reach, disappearing back into the throng of Cuddle Bunny skins.

I swatted them away as I ran through, but Mr. Flopsy-Ears used the skins to his advantage. Punches rained down on me from what seemed like every direction. Every time I yanked one Cuddle Bunny skin from the rack, another shot landed on me from the other side. He was moving too fast.

I battled through the Bunny-skin obstacle course, searching for Mr. Flopsy-Ears, but the constant rattle and hum of the machines disoriented me. I couldn't concentrate.

"Where are you?" I shouted.

I parted two shells to the sides, like I was opening a curtain, only to be met by his little Bunny fist.

He punched me hard.

I staggered back, but recovered in time to see him jump onto the conveyor belt.

He turned back to me and reached into the tear along his seam that I had made earlier. His hand wriggled inside for a moment until he withdrew a vial with red liquid.

"No . . ." I muttered.

He had more potion! He must have only given some of it to Cuddle Bunny Deluxe.

Mr. Flopsy-Ears wiggled his eyebrows and reached for the cork stopper.

"No!" I screamed. I burst through the remaining Bunny skins and leaped onto the conveyor belt after him.

Mr. Flopsy-Ears smirked and scampered away.

I sprinted after him, both of us running against the direction of the conveyor belt, like we were on a factory-length treadmill.

I hopped over oncoming Cuddle Bunnies on the belt, like a sprinter jumping over hurdles, trying to keep in step with Mr. Flopsy-Ears. My strides were longer than his and I started to gain on him.

Ten feet away.

Seven.

Five.

Two.

I lunged for him and managed to snag his tail. "Gotcha!"

Both of us fell forward, landing with a thud on top of the rubbery surface. The vial of potion tumbled from his paw, landing a few feet in front of him. He tried to scramble for it, but I held tight. The motion of the belt sent us moving back toward the direction we had just come from.

In a flash, Mr. Flopsy-Ears twirled around and chomped down on my wrist, sinking his teeth into my flesh.

"Ow!" I screamed, but didn't let go.

With my other hand, I reared back and punched him in the face.

The biting stopped.

My punch also did one other thing . . . it got him mad.

His upper lip curled into a sneer and he bared his Bunny teeth. Before I could react, he leaped on top of me.

The two of us exchanged punches, but he was faster than I was. For every punch I landed, he nailed me three or four times back. And his hurt, while mine didn't seem to have any effect on him at all. Each time I struck him, my fist sank into his stuffed body and bounced off. I hated to say it, but Mr. Flopsy-Ears was stronger than me. I was losing a fight to a stuffed animal. This was not a good way to build my self-esteem.

But there *was* one place where I had him. I was a lot bigger than he was. I needed to use my size to my advantage. I grabbed him by the throat and rolled on top of him.

He twisted away.

My advantage had lasted for probably all of three seconds. He was just too quick.

We tumbled over and over each other, again and again, until he landed back on top. Each of us unleashed a flurry of punches on the other.

He pounded the same spot on my face repeatedly. My eye started to close—I could feel the swelling. My vision blurred.

I couldn't even tell if he was in any pain or not. That was the problem with fighting a stuffed animal. He looked almost exactly the same as when we started.

Out of the corner of my eye, I kept sight of the vial. As long as he was punching me, he wasn't bringing any more

Cuddle Bunnies to life. But I couldn't keep this up for much longer. If I didn't figure something out, and soon, Mr. Flopsy-Ears would finish me off and create a new army of new Cuddle Bunnies. I couldn't let that happen. Ironically enough, the one thing that kept me alert was the rattling of the machines. It was growing louder and louder, until it felt like it was almost right on top of us.

Wait a second . . . *right on top of us?*

Mr. Flopsy-Ears and I both peeked back over our shoulders toward the sound. The giant sewing needle was coming down in a blur and stitching Cuddle Bunnies together. It was way too close.

If I didn't get off this thing, it would nail me right into the belt.

We turned back to each other.

Mr. Flopsy-Ears smiled.

Uh-oh.

I tried to roll off to the side, but he grabbed me tightly.

I pounded on him. "Let go of me!"

We moved toward the needle. The whirring sound grew louder and louder, almost deafening.

Sweat poured down my face, stinging my eyes. I pictured the needle coming down through my body, stabbing into my flesh. Unless I did something fast, I was about to become a human pincushion.

Think, Devin! C'mon, think!

That's when it hit me. It might be my only chance.

I sang.

"I'm a Hugging Hippo, I'm your hugging friend, we'll always be together, I'll follow you to the end."

Mr. Flopsy-Ears recoiled and covered his ears.

That split second of him taking his paws away was all I needed.

"Aaaaaaargh!" I screamed and reached down and grabbed Mr. Flopsy-Ears' legs. Using whatever strength I had left, I flipped him back over my head . . . right at the needle.

Almost instantly, the rhythmic hum of the constant, smooth, stitching sound grew clunky. Choppy. A red light flashed, followed by a loud buzzing. The conveyor belt ground to a halt.

I turned over to see the needle had jammed on the stuffing and lodged itself in Mr. Flopsy-Ears' belly, nailing him to the conveyor belt, like a butterfly pinned in a frame.

He was stuck.

I collapsed onto the belt and took several deep breaths. I turned once more to look at him. He was trying to pull himself free. I eased myself off the belt and onto the floor and nearly collapsed. Everything hurt, but I managed to stay on my feet. I staggered over to where Mr. Flopsy-Ears was.

He was still struggling, but it was no use. He wouldn't be able to get free without shredding himself apart.

The two of us just stared at each other in silence for a few moments.

Finally, I took a step toward him.

His eyes grew wide and he tilted his head to the side. He blinked several times and changed his expression. He looked more . . . innocent. He now looked at me like those cartoon animals, begging for mercy. His ears drooped and hung limply to his sides. His lower lip quivered. He put his little paws together up by his chin and whimpered. All he needed was an eye twinkling and a teardrop falling to complete the effect.

I had to ignore it, and needed to remember all the damage he'd done. All the violence he'd been responsible for. Think how only a few moments ago, he'd tried to kill me. But I couldn't do it. Not with the way he was looking at me.

I clenched my fist and turned away, hating myself for being weak, when I spied something on the conveyor belt. Something I'd almost forgotten about. The vial of red potion.

I reached for it.

Mr. Flopsy-Ears' gaze followed me. When he realized what I was going for, he snarled and reached out. *Thank you for reminding me how evil you were.*

I held the vial up and stared at it before looking back at Mr. Flopsy-Ears. "Is this what you want?"

He trembled and growled, trying to yank himself free from the machine again, but couldn't. His expression changed back again to one of hatred. He bared his teeth.

"Well, too bad!" I threw the vial down and it smashed to pieces, a red puddle oozing out onto the floor.

Mr. Flopsy-Ears' head dropped. His shoulders sagged.

I walked over to him, being careful to stay out of his reach. "I'm going to go outside, get the police, let them take care of you, and then go home to spend Christmas with my family. Goodbye Mr. Flopsy-Ears. I always hated you."

I started to walk away, but stopped and turned back to him. "And one more thing . . . the Hugging Hippo was a much better toy than the Cuddle Bunny will ever be."

I turned and walked out of the factory, ignoring his howls behind me.

CHAPTER TWENTY-THREE

SOCKS FOR EVERYONE

I awoke Christmas morning feeling like I had been pummeled for twenty rounds by Mike Tyson. Actually, I can't imagine Mike Tyson punching harder than Mr. Flopsy-Ears. Even breathing was painful. Normally on Christmas, I'd be the first one down to the tree to open my gifts, but right then, any movement I made sent jolts of pain screaming through my body. My eye was still swollen and it hurt to even blink.

I lay there and thought back to the night before. The rest of it had gone by in a blur.

Once I gave the security guard back his keys that Mr. Flopsy-Ears had stolen, he agreed to radio for help. The FAB Corporation sent their own team down to investigate. It was chaos when they arrived. After speaking to us, they asked Dad and me not to say anything to anyone else until a company representative could come by the next day to get our official statements.

They didn't even let me back inside the factory to see what they did to Mr. Flopsy-Ears. They told me he was finished and would never bother me again. I had to admit, once I heard that, I almost broke down with relief. There was a part of me that regretted not being there for it, but as much as I wanted to see that psycho stuffed animal finally pay for everything he'd done, it was okay with me to let them take care of it on their own. That little bunny scared me, and the less I saw of him, the better.

When I finally did get home, I crashed, but I could honestly say it was the best sleep I'd had since this whole thing started. Not having to worry about any evil Cuddle Bunnies coming to kill me during the night definitely took away a lot of my anxiety.

For the moment, I was perfectly content to just lie there in my bed. Not long, maybe just six or seven months until everything stopped hurting.

"Mooooooooooooom!" Abby screamed.

Well, so much for that.

I jumped out of bed, grabbed my bat, and made my way down the stairs, feeling like an old man as I limped down one step at a time.

When I finally reached the living room, Mom and Dad were already there, searching through the gifts under the tree.

Abby stood off to the side with her head hung low. Her shoulders were slumped. Her bottom lip curled into a pout. She had accomplished the impossible: even I felt bad for her.

"What's going on?" I asked.

Dad stared at me. "What are you holding a bat for?"

I shrugged. "I heard Abby scream. I wanted to be sure she was okay."

"She's fine. You can put the bat away." He resumed searching under the tree. "It's nothing dangerous, but Abby's gift is missing."

I placed the bat against the wall. I had a terrible feeling, but had to ask anyway. "Her gift? What was it?"

"Abby asked Santa for an iPod," Dad said. "And I'm pretty sure I saw that he left her one."

Uh-oh. "Are you sure Santa left *Abby* an iPod?"

Dad stopped searching through the gifts and turned to me. He gave me one of his interrogating looks that he'd used often through the years. "Yes, *Abby*. You wouldn't happen to know anything about it now, would you?"

This was not going to be a fun conversation. "Uh, I didn't know it was for Abby."

He arched an eyebrow. "Does that mean you know where it is?"

I glanced at Abby. "Uh, no . . ."

Abby pointed at me. "He stole my iPod!"

Mom motioned for her to calm down. "Sweetie . . ."

"If he didn't take it, then that means Santa didn't get me anything!" Abby said.

Dad held up his hands. "Okay, everyone stop! I'm sure Devin didn't take it and it's in here somewhere." He stood up holding a small box in his hands. "We'll deal with the iPod in a minute, but first, while you're here . . ." He held the box out to me. "Devin, this is for you."

My hand trembled a bit as I took it from him. "This is mine? What is it?"

"Why don't you open it and find out?" he said.

Mom smiled. "I think you'll like it."

I wasted no time and shredded the paper off to reveal the best gift in the world. What I had been asking for since forever. "You got me an iPhone!"

Abby's jaw dropped. "You gave him an iPhone?"

Mom looked a little uncomfortable. "Well, Santa did."

I didn't care who got it for me. I finally had my iPhone and ran over and threw my arms around Mom and Dad and squeezed hard. "Thank you!"

Dad tousled my hair. "You deserve it. You did good, Dev. I'm proud of you. You were a real hero yesterday."

The doorbell rang.

"I'll get it," Mom said and walked out of the room.

Dad leaned down and whispered in my ear. "You better go find Abby's iPod or this is going to be one very loud and ugly Christmas."

"Dad, I'm not sure where it is," I said, even though I had a bad feeling that I did. I didn't remember taking it from the food court. "I thought it was mine."

"Why would you think it's yours?" he asked. "You asked for an iPhone. And besides, didn't you notice that all the FAB songs were on it?"

I winced. "That's why they were there. I was wondering about that."

Mom walked back into the room, smiling. "Look who's here!"

Tommy hobbled in behind her, on crutches. He had a cast on his leg. "Hey."

I ran over and hugged him, lifting him off the ground. "Tommy! I'm so glad to see you," I said and realized that I meant it. "How are you feeling?"

"Easy!" Tommy said. "One broken bone is enough for me."

"Oh, sorry." I put him down and let go. "I didn't think you were even still coming today."

"I told my mom I still wanted to come for dinner, and since she still had some cooking to do, I asked her to drop me off early, so I could find out everything that happened last night."

Before I could explain, Abby let out a huge shriek from the Christmas tree. "It's not here!" She collapsed to the floor and buried her head in her arms, hysterically crying. "Everyone got what they wanted but me. I don't have a Cuddle Bunny, I don't have an iPod, I don't have a-ny-thing!"

Mom went over to Abby and rubbed her back. "Abby, I'm sure it's here somewhere." She glanced at me. "We just have to find it."

Something was happening that I never thought possible. I really felt bad for Abby. I realized that I'd been responsible for destroying the two things she wanted most for Christmas.

I looked around the room at everyone and thought about how lucky I'd been through all of this. I could've been killed on more than one occasion, yet I was still here. With my family and best friend by my side. And really, nothing else mattered.

I walked over to her. "Abby?"

"Leave me alone!" she said.

I tapped her shoulder. "But I still didn't give you my gift yet."

She lifted her head and wiped her eyes. "Your gift?"

I held out the iPhone to her. "Merry Christmas."

Abby's eyes grew wide. She looked up at me and took the iPhone from my hand. "Really?"

I nodded. "Yeah."

She sprang to her feet and squeezed me tight. "Thank you, thank you, thank you, thank you, thank you!" She raised it above her head like she'd won a prize. "I have an iPhone!" She giggled, but then her eyes narrowed. "I can't wait to tell Lisa. She thought she was so special because she got an Easy-Bake oven. Well, too bad, because I got an iPhone!" She started to run off, but screeched to a halt and turned back to me. She sprinted over and hugged me once again. "I love you, Devin!" She bolted from the room and we heard her bounding up the stairs.

Mom touched my cheek. "Devin, that was very sweet. Don't worry, we'll get you another phone."

Dad's head whipped toward her. "We will? You want me to pay for four cell phone plans?"

Mom glared at him. "It's Christmas, honey."

"But . . ."

Mom's smile disappeared.

Dad sighed. "Fine."

The doorbell rang again.

"Well, this is a busy day," Mom said. "I'll get it."

Tommy hopped over to the couch and sat down. "Now, are you going to tell me what happened or not?"

I started to tell him about everything that happened at the factory, but was interrupted.

"Devin?" Mom's voice from the doorway.

I turned to see her standing there right next to—

"Herb!" I said and looked at Mom. "Why did you let him in here?"

"Devin," Mom said. "Herb would like a chance to explain. I think you should hear him out."

"Well, at least somebody's going to explain," Tommy said.

Herb was dressed in a gray suit and had a bandage wrapped around the top of his head where Mr. Flopsy-Ears had hit him. In his arms, he held several packages.

"Mom," I said. "Herb is evil! We can't trust him! He's the one responsible for all the Cuddle Bunnies to begin with."

Herb wrung his hands. "Devin, I sincerely apologize. You are absolutely right to be upset. I was so focused on getting even with FABCorp that I didn't stop to think about all the potential dangers it might have caused."

I shook my head. "You can't believe anything he says."

"Herb," Mom said. "Maybe it'd be best if you left. I think you're upsetting Devin."

"I agree," Dad said. "You put my family in danger and I don't care if you apologize or not. You need to go."

I looked at Dad. Finally. It felt good to have him not only believe me, but to be on my side as well.

Herb placed his packages down on the floor. "But wait! I didn't just come here to apologize, I also came here in an official capacity." He reached into his jacket pocket, withdrew a card, and handed it to me. It was handwritten. "As you see, I'm also a newly appointed representative of FABCorp, so I took the liberty of creating some business cards for myself. I'll exchange it for you once my regular cards come in."

I examined the card.

HERBERT DORFMAN
REGIONAL VICE-PRESIDENT OF DEVELOPMENT
FABCORP
DORFMEISTER@FABCORP.COM

"I don't have a company phone yet," Herb said. "But they told me they're going to get me one any day."

"They hired you?" I asked. "After all you did to them, they hired you?"

Herb clapped. "Yes, aren't corporations wonderful? In case you haven't seen yet, FABCorp is all over the news today. Everyone thinks this was one big publicity stunt. This was basically free advertising for them. They feel that with my vision and toy expertise, I can help make the next line of FABCorp toys hotter than Bo Derek running on a beach."

"Who?" Tommy and I asked at once.

"Anyhoo," Herb said, "FABCorp wants to make sure there are no hard feelings and have authorized me to offer you a substantial settlement in exchange for your silence as to the events that transpired yesterday." He once again reached into his jacket pocket and this time withdrew a check. He pinched it between two fingers and held it out in front of him.

"Herb," I said. "We don't want anything from you and I'm going to—"

"Did you say substantial?" Dad said. "How much is 'substantial?'"

Herb offered the check to Dad.

Dad took it and held it up in front of his face. His eyes nearly bulged out of their sockets. He turned to Herb. "We accept your apology."

Herb clapped again. "Wonderful!"

"Dad!" I said.

"Everybody deserves a second chance, Dev." Dad shoved the check into his pocket.

Herb smiled at me. "Devin, I promise you, I'm really not a bad guy. I just made a mistake." He held up his index finger. "Wait! I brought something for you too." He scooped up his packages. There were three boxes wrapped in red Christmas paper. "These are for the two of you." He handed one each to me and Tommy and gave the last box to Mom. "And one for dear Abby. Oh, did you hear what I said? Dear Abby. Herb, you are a card sometimes." He laughed.

I had no idea what he was talking about. "Herb, Tommy and I really don't want—"

"What is it?" Tommy tore off the wrapping paper.

I sighed. Was I the only normal one in here?

Tommy waved the box in front of him. "An Elvis Sockley!"

Herb nodded. "Yes, and Devin, you got the crown jewel of the line, the Sockmund Freud."

"Lucky!" Tommy said.

"And Abby got the Joan of Sock, from our historical line," Herb said. "These are just prototypes. FABCorp will begin mass-producing them, and with good marketing, they should be selling like hotcakes by next Christmas!"

So, after all that, it was another Christmas where I'm getting socks. "And what does the sock do? Strangle you? Smother you while you sleep?"

"Oh, dear me, no!" Herb shook his head. "The SOK-P 3000 is not your average sock puppet. It stands for Stimulating and Overly Knowledgeable Pal. Finally, a toy that's not only incredibly adorable, as you can clearly see, but will also be filled with information about the person they represent. And what's more, they can have conversations with not just their human facilitator, but with each other too! Oh, would that I were a child again."

At that moment, I realized that even after everything that had happened, and all that I'd been through, I would never have any clue what this guy was saying.

"In any event," Herb continued, "I'd better get going. I'm sure you all want to be together for Christmas. I'll just mosey over to my house, alone, by myself, without family. I think I might even have some leftover lasagna in the fridge."

Mom looked at me.

I rolled my eyes, but nodded.

Mom smiled. "Herb?"

"I'd love to!" Herb punched the air for emphasis. "Say around three? I'll bring dessert." He turned to me. "And Devin, don't you worry about a thing. I know now that all this unpleasantness is behind us, we're going to get along FAB-ulously." He laughed. "Oh, Herb, you rascal. Anyway, I'll see all of you later!"

"I'll walk you out," Mom said.

They both left the room.

Dad waited a moment until they were gone and turned to me. "Okay, listen up. I'm going to take a nap, but if your mother asks, you tell her I'm upstairs paying bills like she asked, okay?" He rushed out of the room without waiting for an answer.

Tommy tried on his Elvis Sockley and flapped his hands to move the mouth. Its eyes lit up and a familiar voice came out. "Thank you, thank you very much." Tommy laughed. "This is awesome!"

I sighed again.

"Hey, watch it!" a voice from outside.

"What's that?" Tommy propped his crutches under his arms and hobbled over to the window.

I followed him.

Outside, were three guys carrying something from a small truck toward a house. It looked like a coffin. We opened the window to hear better.

"Easy!" one of them said. "This thing is supposed to be valuable."

"Why are we carrying a coffin?" Another asked.

The first guy shrugged. "I don't know. I think the owner is an actor or something, who collects movie memorabilia. Supposedly, an expensive prop. Who cares, really? He's paying us double to move it in on Christmas Day, so I didn't ask any questions."

"It sure is heavy," the third guy said. "Feels like there's already a body in it. Want to take a peek inside?"

The first guy refused. "Nah, they told me that exposure to the sun will destroy the value of the piece."

"Devin?" Tommy whispered.

"Yeah?"

"I don't know how to tell you this, but I think you have a vampire moving in across the street."

I stared at the movers for a few moments, watching them carry the coffin toward the house, before finally turning back to Tommy. "I really hate this town."

THE END

ACKNOWLEDGEMENTS

You're going to have to bear with me. This is my first novel, and it seems like there are so many people to thank, that I almost feel like this should be a book in and of itself. And if the good people over at SkyPony are reading this, I'm perfectly willing to negotiate that into a contract. If it's successful, we can always work that into Acknowledgements: The Sequel. I'll have my agent call you.

And by the way, if it becomes a movie, I'm picturing Will Smith in the lead role.

Anyway, why are my acknowledgments so long, you might be asking?

Well, as I stated above, this is my debut book, and you only get to thank everyone who helped you break in once. So, I want to make sure that I cover everyone, even though I'm pretty sure I'm going to leave someone out. If I do, just know it wasn't intentional . . . well, except for Lester Sherman. I left him out on purpose.

So, since the list is long, I guess I'd better get right to it!

First off, I must start with my Super-Agent, Nicole Resciniti. You believed in me and this book right from the start. Actually, you told me you were hooked from the first page and nothing I had ever heard up until that point thrilled me more. You helped fulfill my dream, and I can never thank you enough for that. You have been there for phone calls of support, strategy and ultimately celebration. I can't imagine anyone having an agent as supportive and nice as you are. And seriously, how many people can say that their agent came out, while pregnant, to watch their daughter play softball, and even bring doughnuts for the team?

I can.

Next, is the trio of editors I've been fortunate to have over at Sky Pony, or the Holy Trinity, as I like to refer to them as. First, was Adrienne Szpyrka, who acquired this book and loved it right from the start. She passed the baton over to Kylie Brien, who helped refine it and also showed a lot of love for it. And finally, Kat Enright, who has shown unparalleled passion and enthusiasm for it, and helped bring it across the finish line. Thank you all so much for making this happen! And by the way, that gratitude extends to everyone else at Sky Pony who had a hand in helping make *Night of the Living Cuddle Bunnies* a reality.

They say writing is a solitary endeavor, but that isn't true. Well, I mean *other* than the hours and hours I spend alone. Still, even with all that alone time taken into account, I've been blessed to be part of a great writing community here in Florida SCBWI. For the most part, this community has been an incredibly supportive one. I've met so many fantastic people who have been instrumental in helping me reach this point. One of the very first was Gloria Rothstein, who offered friendship and advice before anyone else. Thank you, Gloria!

My first critique ever was with Dorian Cirrone, who was kind, gave me great feedback, and tried to guide me along the proper path. She suggested cage fighting but I chose writing instead.

A lot of writers languish forever between that stage of rough draft and polished enough to be published, and I might have done the same if not for Joyce Sweeney. Joyce, you have been an incredible mentor to me and even more importantly, an incredible friend. You've been nurturing and demanding of the writers under your tutelage. And while it's not always easy being your favorite mentee, I still gladly accept the responsibility. And honestly, I never listen to all the things that Faran says, I think you're the best.

My critique group, The Tuesdays, have been instrumental in helping shape *Night of the Living Cuddle Bunnies* to the point where it was in the best shape to be published. And even though I sometimes found your game "Let's make Jonathan cry" a bit much and unnecessary, I realized later after you explained to me that I was just being overly sensitive, that it helped toughen me up, so I could make the manuscript the best it could be. So, big thanks to Joanne Loveday Butcher, Cathy Castelli, Faran Fagen, Melody Maysonet and Stacie Ramey. Stacie, besides being a member of The Tuesdays with me, you have also been a great friend and thank you for being there for all the commiserating through the years. I realize it couldn't have been easy all those years, knowing that Joyce loved me more, yet you never let that come between our friendship, and for that, I thank you.

Writers do like to commiserate and share failures, successes, and stories. I've been fortunate enough to have some great friends from Florida SCBWI to share them all with. Danette Haworth, Jill Mackenzie, Ty Shiver, Cassie Trohn and Mindy Alyse Weiss, thank you for your friendship and support through the years. Also, thank you to Kerry O'Malley Cerra, for always trying to match me with the perfect person to critique my stories. And lastly, to Debbie Reed Fischer, who after several years of honing my writing, critiqued my work and said those magic words, "You're ready." It was a big pick-me-up at that point in my writing life.

To my fellow Swanky, Melissa Roske, it was great to be able to share the debut experience with you at the same time! Hopefully we'll be able to share many more book years and months again in the future!

As far as my non-writing life, thanks to Paul Kallwitz, who promised me twenty dollars to put him in the acknowledgements. If he doesn't pay up, in my next book I'll let everyone know how he lied to me.

To my high school English teacher, Linda Spurny, who won't remember me at all, but made writing fun. She gave me a love of writing by letting us have time to get creative. This was back in the days when students could actually write for fun.

To Eddie Morris. In many ways you were my Tommy growing up. Definitely helped get me out of my shell and push me to do things I might not have done without you. Looking back on it, I'm not so sure if that was a good thing or not.

And to all the people, who have written emails, made phone calls, and messaged me online, asking which is my favorite part of this book? Well, if I had to choose only one, it would be page twenty-four.

To my Mom and Dad, for always believing in me and encouraging me. I got my love of reading from my Dad. He was always in the middle of three or four books at a time. I do the same thing now and have a stack next to the bed. I want you to know, it was a lot of pressure being the favorite to the both of you growing up, but I strongly and bravely dealt with it and hope this made you proud.

To the Snyder and Wexler families, and in particular, my nephews and niece, Avi, Eitan, Oren, Aidan, Spencer and Brynn. Your cuteness will only get you so far. Now, go out and start hawking books to your friends in order to earn Tio's love.

And above all else, thanks to my family. My wife, Michele, thank you for all the sacrifices you've made to allow me to finish this. It wasn't always easy, but you gave me time to work. To my kids, Shaylee, David and Maya, and our dog, Parker. Now you know why Daddy was at the computer all the time, talking to himself. You kids are the best, and in the past year or so, I've come to grow quite fond of all of you. I love you all and hope you're proud of the outcome.